My Back Doesn't Hurt Anymore

My Back Doesn't Hurt Anymore

Simple Techniques for Everyday Pain Prevention

by Jack R. Tessman

quick fox

In Great Britain: Book Sales Ltd., 78 Newman Street, London W1P 3LA.
In Canada: Gage Trade Publishing, P.O. Box 5000, 164 Commander
Blvd., Agincourt, Ontario M1S 3C7.
In Japan: Quick Fox, 2-13-19 Akasaka, Tamondo Bldg., Minato-ku,
Tokyo 107.

Book and cover design by Barry L.S. Mirenburg
Cover photograph by Herbert Wise
Book illustrations by Maurice Whitman

To Lisa and Debbie,
who named it
and pictured it.

To Lora,
whose vital help
was intimate.

Bowed by the weight of centuries he leans
Upon his hoe and gazes on the ground,
The emptiness of ages in his face,
And on his back the burden of the world.

Edwin Markham: *The Man with the Hoe*

Contents

Foreword

My Back Doesn't Hurt Anymore is the most logical, practical and intelligent approach to the problem of back pain available to the general public. While it is directed to the patient who has had recurrent back pain, it is also a must for the *healthy* adult, as preventive medicine. We live in a health-conscious society increasingly concerned about maintaining health via exercise, weight control and dietary intake; Jack Tessman makes a major contribution toward the care and maintenance of one's back.

Jack Tessman's approach to the lower back is from the point of view of a physicist—but don't let that frighten you. By explaining the principle of the lever, as it applies to the back, he tells us why certain activities hurt and others don't. He tells us how to lift, sit, carry, and engage in sex. Herein is the simple and elegant logic of this book: from the principle of the lever to the care of one's precious back.

His review of the anatomy of the back is concise, accurate, and fairly technical. But there is nothing here that cannot be easily understood from the ample diagrams. Certainly if one has a back problem, then a knowledge of terminology would be invaluable in talking to a physician or physical therapist.

Many authors make the error of advocating one or another of the numerous fads for back pain. Jack Tessman lists the fads, and tells us again of how the simple principle of the lever and how your daily activities affect the pressure on your discs. He reminds his reader that the decision as to what will be done for your back, and to your back, is entirely the decision of the sufferer.

I would urge the reading of this book *before* one has a back problem. As presented here by Jack Tessman, the care and respect offered to one's deserving back could well prevent a lot of pain and suffering and operations.

GARY KORENMAN, M.D.
Neurologist at St. Luke's and Mt. Sinai hospitals in New York City

Introduction

How do I, a physicist, come to write a book on low back pain? I, too, have suffered from back pain, as have so many others. I can tell the usual tale.

One summer day, in a cottage on Cape Cod, I awoke and found that I couldn't get out of bed. Every time I tried it, I was stopped by an onslaught of intense pain in the lower back. I recalled that the day before, I had leaned over a safety gate—the kind put across a stairway to prevent young children from tumbling down—picked up one of my daughters, and lifted her over the gate. I had felt a twinge at the time and had thought, "I shouldn't have done that." I finally managed to crawl out of bed and get myself to a physician. He diagnosed a muscle spasm, prescribed a muscle relaxant and a pain suppressor, and in a day, the situation was much improved.

A couple of days later we had to move out to make way for the next tenant. There were a number of heavy boxes to be carried out to the station wagon. It just had to be done, and since my back had improved, I was the one who did it. I carried them out on my back, as was my usual way of carrying heavy loads, and experienced no difficulties.

I had had back troubles before, but these two events coming so close together made me curious. Why were there such different consequences from lifting the child one way and from carrying the boxes another way?

Thus began my inquiry into the biomechanics of the spine and my study of recent excellent research on low back pain. The subject is particularly susceptible to understanding and analysis by a physicist because, in addition to the biological and possibly psychological factors, an extremely important role is played by the mechanics of the spine by the forces that are brought to bear when the various muscles and tissues act to support the tasks of daily activities, even such activities as sitting in a chair. Here, then, is one area of body care, the alleviation of low back pain, where the physicist has something worthwhile to offer and you have much to gain.

The medical literature reports that about 65% of the acute episodes of low back pain clear up within three weeks and another 25% within two months no matter what therapeutic program you follow—or don't follow. Quite possibly it does not matter what you do because the pain prevents you from doing too many wrong things, so the body has a chance to heal itself. But unfortunately, that healing is not the end of the problem. The pain usually recurs—once, twice, many times—and you may even become one of those for whom the pain does not relent.

The purpose of this book is to help *prevent* the pain from occurring. I'd like to say: to help prevent the pain from occurring in the first place. But I strongly suspect that until you have had at least one experience of back pain, you are unlikely to be convinced that you need to work to prevent it. So more realistically, I hope you will use this book at least to help avoid the re-occurrence of pain.

The middle chapters of the book discuss and illustrate in detail how to go about the activities of everyday living: what to do and not to do in the home, at work, in the garden, at play, in bed, standing, sitting, driving, shopping.

The early chapters briefly discuss the anatomy and mechanics of the back and establish the reasons for the instructions that follow. Chapters 1 and 11 discuss some of the supporting research work.

Perhaps the middle chapters contain all the information you want from this book, or all you have time for. However, if you're like me, you may wish to know the reasons. This knowledge may make it easier for you to organize the do's-and-don'ts in your mind and to remember them. It will also help you handle situations which are not discussed in the book.

JACK R. TESSMAN
Professor of Physics, Tufts University,
Medford, Mass.

1 A Brief Anatomy of the Back

1

A Brief Anatomy of the Back

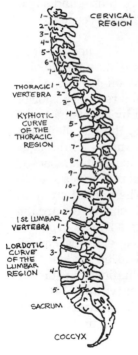

CERVICAL REGION

1-
2-
3-
4-
5-
6-
7-

THORACIC VERTEBRA 1-
2-
3-

KYPHOTIC CURVE OF THE THORACIC REGION
4-
5-
6-
7-
8-
9-
10-
11-
12-

1st LUMBAR VERTEBRA 1-
2-

LORDOTIC CURVE OF THE LUMBAR REGION
3-
4-
5-

SACRUM

COCCYX

Fig. 1–1. The vertebras of the spine, showing the lordotic curve of the lumbar region and the kyphotic curve of the thoracic region.

A little knowledge of anatomy, specifically the structure of the back, will help us understand how the back functions and what may go wrong. Add a little knowledge of the elementary mechanics of the lever and we can begin to understand how to help prevent some of the troubles.

THE SPINE

The core structure of the back is the spine (Fig. 1–1). It supports the entire upper portion of the body and at the same time provides the flexibility that allows the body to bend in all directions. It consists of twenty-four segments, each of which contains a bone called a *vertebra*. The vertebras are stacked one on top of the other, but not directly. Between every two vertebras is a soft, flexible, cushioning material called the *intervertebral disc*—the famous disc. We shall have much to say about it.

The spine may be divided into three regions. At the top is the cervical or neck region consisting of seven vertebras and their accompanying discs. (*Cervix* simply means neck. You may be more accustomed to hearing it used in reference to a portion of the female reproductive system. In that context, it means the neck of the uterus.) The cervical spine supports the head, and the flexibility of the cervical spine permits the wide range of motion of which the head is capable.

Next is the thoracic or chest region. The thoracic

spine contains twelve vertebras, with a pair of ribs fastened to each.

Below that is the lumbar region—the lower back. This is the principal problem region and it is here that we will concentrate our attention. Here we experience low back pain. Here too may be the source of irritations that the brain interprets and we experience as a pain in the buttocks, thigh, or leg.

The lumbar spine contains five vertebras and their discs. Counting from the top down, the vertebras are referred to as the first lumbar vertebra, the second lumbar vertebra, and so on—or just simply the L1 vertebra, the L2 vertebra, and so on. The discs below each vertebra are, correspondingly, called the L1 disc, the L2 disc, . . .

These twenty-four vertebras of the cervical, thoracic, and lumbar regions constitute the flexible portion of the spine. They rest on the large, triangular sacrum bone which is the rear or posterior region of the pelvic area, joined by ligaments to the neighboring bones of the pelvis, the left ilium and the right ilium, more familiarly known as the hips.

The spine is not a straight vertical column. Looked at from the side, it is curved, and the curves are different in each of the regions. The normal curve of the spine in the thoracic region is convex toward the rear. This type of curve is referred to as *kyphotic*. The normal curve of the lumbar spine is convex toward the front and referred to as *lordotic*. We shall see later that, in various situations, the lumbar spine may take on different curvatures. It may become more lordotic, less lordotic, or even kyphotic, and we shall have to consider what that does for back troubles.

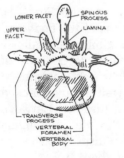

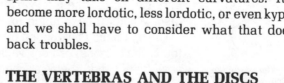

Fig. 1-2.   A lumbar vertebra viewed from above and from the side.

THE VERTEBRAS AND THE DISCS

Let's look at an individual vertebra and disc (Fig. 1-2). The bulk of the vertebra is the front portion, the vertebral body. It is cylindrical, with flat oval-shaped top and bottom surfaces. It, along with the disc, carries the load imposed upon the spine.

The rear portion of the vertebra includes three prominently projecting pieces of bone, two of them

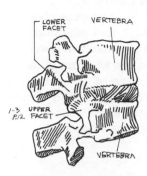

Fig. 1-3. Side view showing front and rear portions of two vertebras and an intervertebral disc.

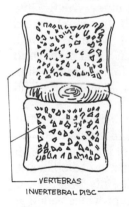

VERTEBRAS
INVERTEBRAL DISC

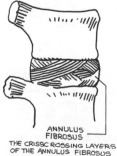

ANNULUS FIBROSUS
THE CRISSCROSSING LAYERS OF THE ANNULUS FIBROSUS

Fig. 1-4. Cross sections and side view of two vertebras and an intervertebral disc.

projecting sideways and called the *transverse processes*, and one projecting rearward, called the *spinous process*. The spinous processes are the "buttons" that you can see and feel running down the middle of your back. The rear portion of the vertebra provides places for the attachment of ligaments and muscles.

In addition, the rear portion of the vertebra includes two upper and two lower surfaces which are nearly flat and are called *facets*. The lower facets of one vertebra glide along the upper facets of the vertebra below. Thus the facets guide and limit the motion of one vertebra relative to its neighboring vertebra. The facets of the lumbar vertebras are in a vertical plane and their arrangement allows the lumbar spine to bend forward and backward but restricts sideways bending; whereas the facets of the thoracic vertebras restrict forward and backward bending but permit sideways bending and rotation or twisting around the vertical axis. Working together, as they do, the thoracic and lumbar regions of the spine allow the body its large range of movement.

Between the vertebras are the intervertebral discs (Figs. 1-3 and 1-4). Compared to an adjacent vertebra, a disc has approximately the same cross-sectional shape and about one-third the thickness. The circumferential wall of a disc is a mesh of tough, elastic, diagonally crisscrossing fibers firmly fastened, above and below, to the adjacent vertebras. The full name of this wall is *annulus fibrosus*, but we'll call it simply the *annulus*. The interior of the disc contains a gel-like fluid and is called the *nucleus pulposis*, or just the *nucleus*.

The upper and lower faces of the discs are not parallel. Instead, each disc is appropriately wedge-shaped; some are thinner in front, some thinner toward the rear. All together they give the spine its natural curve—the lumbar lordosis and thoracic kyphosis.

But the spine is not restricted to its natural curves. The disc, with its fluid nucleus and flexible, fibrous annulus, permits each vertebra to tilt forward or backward, or side to side, or even twist, relative to the vertebra below. The discs are what make the spine a jointed, segmented structure capable of so much flexibility.

The disc is a tough structure which can withstand heavy loads. Sometimes the load can be as high as 600 or 700 pounds, although that may be excessive. Of course, our bodies do not weigh that much and we never pick up or carry packages anywhere near that heavy. But as we shall see, when we examine a little bit of body mechanics and some of the results of disc experiments, the compressive load on the spine can easily be that high in the course of fairly ordinary activities. And then we can get into trouble.

LIGAMENTS

So far, we have described a collection of rigid vertebral bones, piled one on top of the other with flexible discs between them. Left by itself, this stack would promptly topple over, even if it weren't curved. Something is needed to keep it erect and stable and to allow it to bend in a controlled fashion and to support loads. That something is the ligaments and muscles.

A *ligament* is a band of tissue much like a leather thong. It attaches from one bone to another. A ligament is passive tissue. When completely slack, it exerts no pull nor can it be activated to contract. There is tension in a ligament only when it is stretched, and then the support it provides requires no expenditure of energy. It may already be somewhat taut when the bones it connects are in their normal position. This prevents the separation from becoming excessive. When a ligament is stretched too far, it tears. The bones it connected may take on unusual arrangements in relation to each other, because they are no longer restricted and protected by the damaged ligament.

We need concern ourselves here with only the anterior and the posterior longitudinal ligaments (Fig. 1-5). The anterior longitudinal ligament attaches to the front portions of the vertebral bodies and their discs along the entire length of the spine.

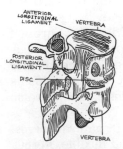

Fig. 1-5. The anterior and posterior longitudinal ligaments.

The posterior longitudinal ligament attaches to the rear portions. Together, they completely enclose the vertebral bodies and the intervertebral discs, meshing with and reinforcing the annulus of each disc— except in the lumbar region. At the first lumbar vertebra, the posterior longitudinal ligament begins to narrow and, in its descent, by the time it reaches the fifth lumbar vertebra it is about one-half its original width and covers only the central posterior portion of the vertebra.

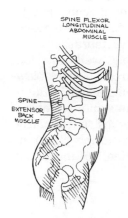

SPINE FLEXOR
LONGITUDINAL
ABDOMINAL
MUSCLE

SPINE
EXTENSOR
BACK
MUSCLE

Fig. 1-6. The muscles that flex the back (bend it forward) and the muscles that extend the back (bend it backward).

MUSCLES

More than eighty muscles act upon the segments of the spine. Because they are so numerous and their Latin names are not familiar words, it will be sufficient, for our purposes, to group them together in a few broad categories and to refer to them by simple descriptive terms (Fig. 1-6).

One group of muscles runs back of the spine, along its entire length, and attaches below, to the sacrum and ilia (hip) bones of the pelvis and above, to the transverse and sinous processes of the vertebras. We shall call it the *back muscle*. Tension in the back muscle tends to bend the spine backwards.

Most people think of the abdomen as completely separate from the back. But the longitudinal abdominal muscle which runs along the front of the abdomen from the lower front bones of the pelvis to the ribs is quite important to the operation of the back. The ribs, remember, are attached to the spine. Thus, when the longitudinal abdominal muscle contracts, it tends to bend the body forward.

Many muscles participate in bending the body sideways. A couple of important muscle groups run on each side, from the spine to the top of the hip bone and to the top of the thigh bone. We shall call these muscles simply the *lateral muscles*.

THE SPINAL CANAL

Between the front and rear portions of each vertebra is an opening. When all the openings are aligned, a

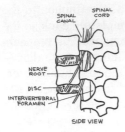

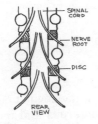

Fig. 1-7. The spinal cord runs almost the full length of the spinal canal, and nerve roots emerge from it laterally between every pair of adjacent vertebras.

Fig. 1-8. An excessive load can cause cracks to develop in the end plate of a vertebra and in the body of the vertebra.

tunnel is formed, running the entire length of the spine. This is the *spinal canal,* and through it runs the *spinal cord* (Fig. 1-7). The spinal cord is a bundle of nerve fibers connecting the brain with all parts of the body and carrying messages to and from the brain. At each vertebral level, nerve roots emerge from the spinal cord and leave the canal through horizontal openings between the vertebras.

The spinal cord is reasonably well-protected within its flexible canal. It requires a severe blow from outside to intrude upon it and damage it. But it is possible for malfunctions of the spine, vertebras or discs to impinge upon the nerves, particularly where they leave the spinal canal. Possibly rigid tunnels would provide better protection, but then we'd all be stiff as ram-rods.

BE KIND TO YOUR DISC

And now, back to the disc. During the first fifteen to twenty years of life, there is a blood supply to and from the disc. Nutrients are furnished, waste products are removed, and the nucleus and annulus are kept in good condition. They are in their prime. But then the blood supply gradually disappears. Without it, nutrients enter and waste products leave the nucleus only by the very slow passage of fluid through the end plates of the adjacent vertebras and through the annulus. The quality of the nucleus and the annulus deteriorates, the fibers of the annulus become more susceptible to damage, and damage is very slow to heal or may not heal at all.

The discs and vertebras are very strong. But there are limits to the compressive loads they can withstand. If they are overtaxed, various events may occur which may cause pain.

An end plate of a vertebra may develop tiny cracks, and the nucleus of the adjacent attached disc may seep in (Fig. 1-8). The combination of cracks and seepage can affect sensory nerve endings in the vertebra and cause pain.

The annulus of the disc may develop small tears

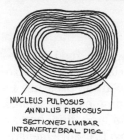

NUCLEUS PULPOSUS
ANNULUS FIBROSUS
SECTIONED LUMBAR
INTRAVERTEBRAL DISC

Fig. 1-9. As a person gets older, tears may occur in the annulus of the disc.

which, though they might not go all the way through the annulus and permit the nucleus to leak out, may allow the nucleus to seep into the annulus (Fig. 1-9). There are sensory nerve endings in the outer portion of the annulus and these may then cause pain.

The fourth and fifth lumbar discs are covered in front by the anterior ligament, but they are only partly covered and reinforced in back by the weaker posterior ligament. The rear side portions of the annulus of the disc are particularly vulnerable. If the annulus becomes weakened and the pressure in the nucleus is high, the nucleus may force the annulus to protrude into the spinal canal and press against a nerve root exiting from the canal through the intervertebral foramen (the opening between the vertebras).

The nerve roots emerging from the lower lumbar region go off to the lower back, buttocks, thighs, legs, and feet. They convey to the brain sensations from these regions. If a nerve is irritated, as by a protruding annulus, it will produce the sensation of pain which seems to originate in the buttocks, thigh, or whatever portion of the leg is served by that nerve. This is commonly called sciatica; it can be very painful.

Not only may a weakened annulus protrude, but it may actually rupture and permit nuclear material to leak out into the spinal canal, irritate nerve roots, and cause the pain of sciatica. This is sometimes called a "slipped disc." But the term slipped disc conjures up an image of a loose, coin-like disc which has slipped out from between the vertebras and must be put back into its proper place. Actually the disc is very securely attached to the adjacent vertebras and cannot slip out from between them. What does happen then? The annulus ruptures and allows the nucleus pulposis to extrude. *Ruptured* or *herniated disc* would be better terms to describe this.

The moral of all this is BE KIND TO YOUR DISC. Don't overload it. Throughout the book, we will examine activities that overload the disc and describe ways to avoid overload.

DISC RESEARCH

In 1964, Dr. Alf Nachemson of Sweden and Dr. James Morris of the United States carried out some extraordinary research. They measured the pressure inside the vertebral discs of living human beings. Guided by x-rays, they inserted a long, thin, hollow, liquid-filled needle, connected to a pressure measuring device, through the back and into the nucleus pulposis of a lumbar disc.

Since then, Dr. Nachemson and co-workers have improved upon the original technique and have continued the studies in Sweden. By now, many measurements have been made of the pressure inside the lumbar discs of a large number of subjects in a variety of different positions and activities: sitting, standing, walking, bending forward, bending sideways, lifting weights, lying down, coughing, laughing, exercising, and so on.

The results are extremely important, both as a confirmation or denial of theoretical expectations and as a guide to those situations which may be helpful or detrimental to the prevention of low back pain.

The studies show that the pressure in the lumbar discs is less when standing than when sitting and least of all when lying down. The pressure is very high when a person bends forward and holds or picks up a weight. Most of this is quite familiar. It is what we would have expected. But it helps to see it confirmed.

Figures 1–10 and 1–11 show some of the results in graphic form. In Fig. 1–10, the approximate load on the third lumbar disc, for various positions of the body, is compared with the load while standing. If we assign the value of 100% to the load on the disc while standing upright and holding nothing, then the load while lying flat on one's back is only 45%. But when sitting, unsupported, the load is greater, about 145%. Bending forward 20° brings the value up to about 170%, and holding 10 kilograms (22 pounds) in each hand while bent over 20° sends the load up to about 265%. Keep in mind that 22 pounds is about the weight of a medium-sized suitcase. Worse yet is

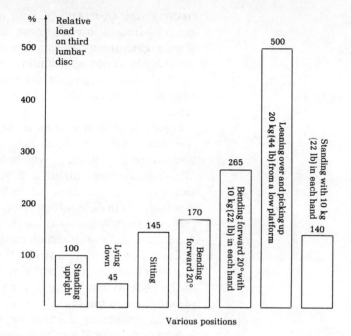

Fig. 1-10. The approximate load on the third lumbar disc, for various positions of the body, compared with the load while standing upright and holding nothing.

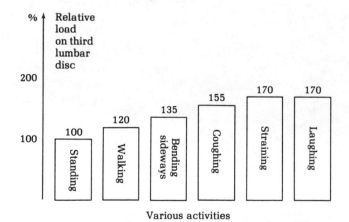

Fig. 1-11. The approximate load on the third lumbar disc, during various activities, compared with the load while standing.

Figs. 1-10 and 1-11 adapted from Alf Nachemson, *Rheumatology and Rehabilitation* 14:129, 1975.

leaning way over and picking up 20 kilograms (44 pounds) from a low platform. The load on the disc shoots up to about five times as much as when standing free! By contrast, standing upright and just holding 10 kilograms in each hand raises the load on the disc to only about 140% of the value when standing free.

Figure 1–11 shows some more relative loads upon the disc during various human activities—again compared to standing which is taken as 100%. Walking produces about a 20% increase; bending sideways, an increase of 35%; coughing, 55%; straining, as in defecating, 70%; laughing, also 70% ("It only hurts when you laugh!").

Another test result which confirmed expectations is that when standing upright, the pressure in a lumbar disc is much greater if a weight is held in front of the body at arm's length than if it is held in front of but close to the body.

If you remember the last time you had a bout of low back pain, or if you're having such trouble right now, you'll recognize that the activities that produce high disc pressure are also the ones that usually cause pain.

2 Some Elementary Mechanics as Applied to the Back

2

Some Elementary Mechanics as Applied to the Back

A little bit of elementary mechanics can help you understand what circumstances may overload the vertebras and discs. This knowledge can also help you understand how you can still do most of the things you want to do *without* overloading the discs.

THE SEESAW

Let's start with this familiar piece of playground equipment. The seesaw is simply a wooden plank resting on a narrow support, around which it can pivot.

Suppose Marjorie Daw, weighing 50 pounds, sits on one end of the seesaw, and Jeffrey, also 50 pounds, on the other end (Fig. 2-1). The seesaw balances. The support holds up both Marjorie and Jeffrey and therefore has to push up on the plank with a force of 100 pounds. (We're ignoring whatever weight the plank itself might have.)

We don't actually need Jeffrey to balance Marjorie on the seesaw. We can simply tie a rope to his end of the seesaw and pull down on it with a force of 50 pounds, or just tie the rope to the ground and let the ground do the pulling (Fig. 2-2). Marjorie is held up, although she isn't able to seesaw. Again the plank presses against the support with a 100 pound force and the support pushes back with a 100 pound force.

If Jeffrey is not around, Marjorie's father, who weighs 150 pounds, can substitute for him. But he will have to sit closer to the support, or pivot (Fig. 2-3). If Marjorie sits 6 feet away from the pivot, her

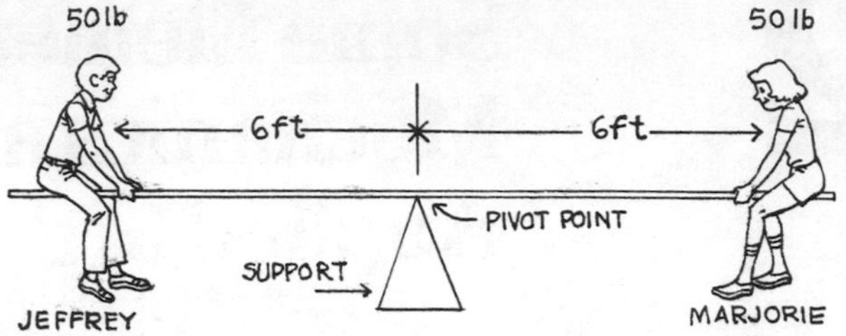

50 lb   50 lb

Fig. 2-1. Marjorie and Jeffrey balance, and together they push against the support with a force of 100 pounds.

JEFFREY   MARJORIE

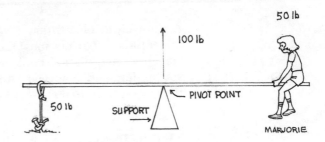

Fig. 2-2. The pull of the rope keeps Marjorie balanced, and again a force of 100 pounds is exerted against the support.

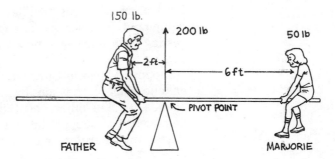

Fig. 2-3. Marjorie is balanced by her father, but now they exert a force of 200 pounds against the seesaw support.

father must sit 2 feet away. The point is that Marjorie's tendency to cause the plank to rotate depends not just on her weight but also on her distance from the pivot. We have to multiply the two quantities together, and we get 50 lb × 6 ft = 300 lb-ft. This is called a *torque*, and it is a measure of the tendency of the plank to turn. In this case, because Marjorie is seated on the right end, the plank would turn in a clockwise direction around the pivot. For Marjorie and her father to balance the plank successfully, her father must cause the same torque around the pivot, but in the opposite direction—counter-clockwise. His 150 pounds at a distance of 2 feet from the pivot produces the necessary torque of 300 lb-ft.

However, the plank is now pressed against the support not with a force of 100 pounds, but 200 pounds, that being the combined weight of Marjorie and her father.

Again, for Marjorie's father, we could substitute a rope, attached 2 feet from the pivot and pulling down with a force of 150 pounds. Marjorie would be balanced and the force on the seesaw support would be 200 pounds.

Let's take just one more variation on the seesaw theme. Playing all by herself, Marjorie can sit directly over the pivot. The seesaw will balance and would press on the support with a force of just 50 pounds.

What these examples show is that there are different ways of supporting Marjorie's weight on the seesaw, and the different ways result in different loads on the seesaw support.

TORQUE

Actually, calculating torques is a little more complicated than the previous examples suggest. Let's look at a different case.

Suppose you want to remove one of the nuts or bolts that keeps the wheel fastened to your car. You use a wrench to apply a counter-clockwise torque. Let's say the wrench is 12 inches long and you apply the torque by pushing down on the wrench with a

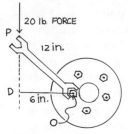

Fig. 2-4.   Pushing against a wrench to undo a wheel bolt. The lever arm is 6 inches.

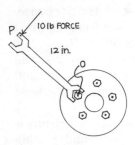

Fig. 2-5.   Here the lever arm is 12 inches.

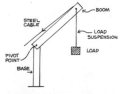

Fig. 2-6.   The steel cable is trying to rotate the boom counter-clockwise around the pivot point while the load and the weight of the boom is urging the boom to rotate clockwise.

force of 20 pounds at point P (Fig. 2-4). The extended line along which the force acts (line PD in the diagram), is called the *line of action* of the force. Point O, the center of the nut, is the pivot point. The shortest distance, from point O to the line of action of the 20 pound force, is the distance OD which is 6 inches. This distance is called the *lever arm.*

In calculating the torque of the 20 pound force, it doesn't matter that point P, where the force is applied, is 12 inches from the pivot. The torque is *not* 20 lb × 12 in. What does matter is the 6 inch length of the lever arm. *Torque is the force multiplied by the lever arm.* In this case, the torque is 20 lb × 6 in. = 120 lb-in. It is a measure of the tendency of the 20 lb force to turn the nut. The greater the torque, the greater the turning tendency.

We could produce the same torque of 120 lb-in. by applying a force of only 10 pounds, but we would have to apply the force perpendicular to the wrench at point P (Fig. 2-5). The distance of OP would then be the lever arm and 10 lb × 12 in. = 120 lb-in. Once again, there are different ways of applying the same torque, and the different ways involve different applied forces.

THE CRANE

As a last mechanical example, one that begins to approach the human situation, let's consider a power crane (Fig. 2-6). A rigid boom is connected to a base at a pivot point O, and the boom is free to rotate around the pivot point. A steel cable is attached to the boom and supports both the boom and a suspended load.

The weight of the boom and of the suspended load both produce torques that tend to rotate the boom clockwise about the pivot point O. The tension in the steel cable pulls on the boom at point A and produces a torque that tends to rotate the boom counter-clockwise. In equilibrium, the counter-clockwise torque must equal the clockwise torques. However, because the cable runs so very close to the pivot point O, the lever arm from O to the cable is very small and the tension in the cable must be extremely large to produce the required torque.

A further consequence is that the weight of the boom and the suspended load, and especially the tension in the steel cable, press the boom against the base with an extremely large force. If the bearing surfaces between the boom and the base are not strong enough, they may be crushed and injured.

Let's put in some numbers and see what the situation is. Suppose the boom weighs 200 pounds and the suspended load is 400 pounds. The boom's weight of 200 pounds is equivalent to a force of 200 pounds pulling down at the center of gravity of the boom. Using the dimensions shown in Fig. 2–7, the 200 pound force acts at a lever arm distance of 6 feet and the 400 pound load at a lever arm distance of 10 feet. Thus, the clockwise torque is 200 lb × 6 ft + 400 lb × 10 ft = 5200 lb-ft. If the distance from the pivot point O to the line of the steel cable is only 1 foot, then the steel cable has to pull with a force of 5200 pounds to produce a counter-clockwise torque of 5200 lb ft. This seems an enormous amount of force to support a boom and load weighing a total of only 600 pounds! The reason for this is the short 1 foot lever arm distance from the pivot to the cable.

The effect of the three forces acting upon the boom—the 400 pound load, the boom's 200 pound weight, and particularly the 5200 pound tension in the cable—is to press the boom against the base with a force in excess of 5200 pounds, even though the crane is only holding up a 400 pound load.

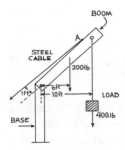

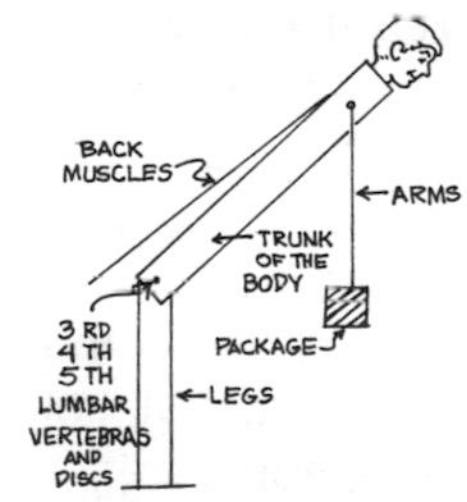

Fig. 2–7. The tension in the steel cable must be very large because the lever arm to the cable is only 1 foot.

THE HUMAN BODY

Now if we draw a small line at the bottom of the base, a head at the end of the boom, and a few flourishes, the crane begins to approximate, roughly, a bent-over person lifting up a package (Fig. 2–8).

The crane's base becomes the person's legs, thighs, and, to some extent, the pelvis; the boom becomes the trunk of the body; the package hangs from the arms; and the crane's steel cable becomes the back muscles. The pivot point becomes the

Fig. 2–8. The human crane.

region around the third, fourth, and fifth lumbar vertebras and the corresponding discs.

Because the lever arm distance to the back muscles is very small, about two inches, the back muscles must pull very hard to hold up the bent-over body and any additional objects your arms may be holding. Just as in the crane's cable, the force the back muscles must exert is far greater than the weight of the bent-over body and the load on the arms.

The back muscles are very strong and can usually, without difficulty, exert the necessary pull. But, as a consequence, the lower vertebras and discs are very strongly compressed; they may be overloaded and cause low back pain. The overloading of the discs does not occur because the back muscles are weak but on the contrary because they are very strong and pull very, very hard on the spine.

As previously stated, the back muscles are mostly in back of the spine. Other muscles, such as the lateral and abdominal muscles, pull, directly or indirectly, upon the spine. However, these other muscles act at larger lever arm distances from the lower vertebras. Therefore they do not have to pull as hard to produce a large torque and do not put as great a load on the lower vertebras and discs.

We must be particularly wary of those activities that require the back muscles to pull very hard. Unlike the flexing of our arm muscles which we are often consciously aware of, the back muscles will act whenever the situation requires it and we are usually quite unaware of what they are up to. It's not easy to tell your back muscles to turn off when doing so will cause you to fall flat on your face.

The only way the back muscles will pull less is to demand less of them. The guiding principle thus becomes: AVOID SITUATIONS THAT IMPOSE LARGE FORWARD-BENDING TORQUES UPON THE UPPER BODY.

3

The Back in Motion:
Basics of Lifting
and Carrying

3

The Back in Motion: Basics of Lifting and Carrying

LIFTING FROM THE FLOOR

Fig. 3-1. "All I did was bend over and pick up a paper clip!"

A friend of mine, in describing what brought on his last attack of low back pain, remarked, "All I did was bend over and pick up a paper clip!" He said it as though that paper clip was the "straw" that broke his back. Of course it wasn't the paper clip; his own weight, his bent-over back, was far heavier (Fig. 3-1).

The weight of his body, way out there in front of his sacrum, resulted in a large torque, around the

Fig. 3-2. A heavy package out there in front of you makes it worse. Don't do this.

Fig. 3-3. You may bend over if you support your body by pushing against a chair or table.

Fig. 3-4. Support your back with your forearm on your knee.

lumbar discs, tending to bend the body forward. To counteract this, to keep his back from falling forward, his back muscles automatically exerted a huge force necessary to develop a counteracting torque. That huge force causes the pressure in the discs to increase and may overload them.

Of course, if you're picking up a package (Fig. 3-2) heavier than a paper clip, the additional torque of the package will aggravate the situation further.

There are safe ways to pick up an object from the floor. It is all right to bend over, providing you support the weight of your upper body by placing your hand on a chair seat or on a low table (Fig. 3–3) and pushing hard. That way, your arm supports your bent-over body, your back muscle can relax, and the disc is not overloaded. When you straighten up, do it with your hand and arm, not with your back muscles.

If there is no support handy, use your knee. Place your hand or forearm on it (Fig. 3–4) and push.

Another safe approach is to keep your back straight and vertical and reach the floor by bending your knees (Fig. 3–5). Here again, the back muscle is not called upon to do anything extra. By not showing its strength, it will not overload your disc.

Fig. 3–5.   Keep your back vertical and bend at the knees.

CARRYING

As far as your back is concerned, a good way to carry things is on it—on your back or behind it—especially for heavy loads.

In Fig. 3–6 a man is correctly carrying a large heavy box on his back. His body is leaning forward, but that's all right in this case because the combined center of gravity of the box and the upper body is almost directly above the lumbar vertebras. All is in equilibrium. There is no torque tending to bend the body further forward, and the back muscle is not called upon to exert any force other than that needed to maintain the stability of the vertebral column. Of course, the lumbar discs must support the weight of the box, but that is far less than the load the discs would have to bear if the back muscle had to get into the act exerting additional force on the vertebras and discs.

The box doesn't have to be carried on the back. It may be more convenient to carry it behind you, hanging down from your arms (Fig. 3–7). The purpose is the same: You will automatically lean forward and the combined center of gravity of the upper body and the box will be directly over the lumbar discs, and thus the load on the discs will be minimized.

It may look funny to the unknowledgeable onlooker

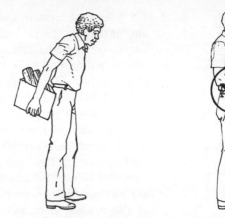

Fig. 3-6. A good way to carry a heavy load—on your back.

Fig. 3-7. Another good way—in back of you. 
Fig. 3-8. Avoid carrying a heavy package in front of you.

Fig. 3-9. Moderately heavy bundles may be carried close to your side—preferably one at each side.

who sees you carrying a box behind you instead of in front (Fig. 3-8), as most people do. But you can be smug in the knowledge that you are being kind to your disc. Perhaps when others catch on, they will do what you do.

A back pack is great. Not only does it free your hands but it places the load where it belongs. It's becoming increasingly popular among school and college kids. Use one when you can. It makes sense.

It may not be convenient to carry a smaller package behind you nor is it really necessary. Instead, carry it close to your side. Carrying approximately equal loads on both sides is best (Fig. 3-9). Once again, that puts the center of gravity of the two loads directly over the lumbar discs, where it belongs.

If the load is carried on only one side or on a shoulder, usually you will automatically lean the body to the opposite side (Fig. 3-10), putting the combined center of gravity over the lumbar discs. If you don't lean to the opposite side, or don't lean enough, then the lateral muscle has to exert a torque on your spine to offset the sideways bending torque exerted by the load. However, the lateral muscles act at a larger lever arm distance from the lumbar discs than do the back muscles. Therefore, when the load is carried at the side, the lateral muscles don't have to pull as hard as the back muscles would if the load were carried in front.

Fig. 3–10. A bundle at your right side is balanced by leaning the body to the left.

Fig. 3–11. If you do carry something in front, keep it close to the body. It helps further if you lean back at the hips.

A pregnant woman *must* carry her baby in front but, of course, it's very close. Even so, the position is tough on her back. The rest of us should try to avoid carrying anything in front for this is the least desirable position. However, if you must then be sure to carry it as close to the body as possible (Fig. 3–11); never carry it way out in front. That way, you will minimize the torque tending to rotate the body forward. Or go even further—carry the object close to the body and at the same time lean backwards at the hips. But be careful because not all the ways of leaning backwards are good. Avoid leaning backwards at the ankles. It makes walking somewhat clumsy and shifts the weight of the legs backwards a bit. We do not want to shift the weight of the *lower* part of the body backwards. What we want, if possible, is to distribute the combined weight of the *upper* part of the body and the object you are carrying so that their center of gravity is directly over the lower lumbar discs.

Also avoid arching the spine backwards. This position increases the curve of the lumbar spine appreciably, exaggerating the lumbar lordosis, and it can raise the pressure in the discs because it distorts their shape. It's also a somewhat awkward posture to maintain.

The effective and safe way to lean backwards is at the hips. The upper portion of the pelvis, and the spine along with it, will move backwards when the hip sockets swivel around the thigh bones in the hip joints. It's easy to do when you're holding a heavy object in front of you next to the body. This position brings the combined center of gravity over the lower lumbar discs, making it unnecessary for the back muscles to act.

LIFTING AND CARRYING AT WORK

If your work requires you to lift heavy things day in and day out, that does not make you less susceptible to low back pain. On the contrary, you're probably more vulnerable, especially if your lifting and carrying technique is not good. Remember, don't lift or carry things in front of your body if it can be avoided. If you must, then lift or carry the object as close to your body as possible. But it's better to carry it in back of you or at your side. Get another worker to help you, and carry heavy objects between you, one at each side. Best of all, use wheels, use power lifts.

I witnessed an excellent demonstration of proper lifting technique on the job. At an airline check-in

Fig. 3-13.   DON'T bend over and pick the suitcase up in front of you.
Fig. 3-14.   Don't switch hands with the suitcase in front of you. Switch hands in back of you.

counter recently, I watched with great pleasure as the woman attendant picked up a suitcase with superb style and placed it on the conveyor belt. She bent her knees, kept her back vertical, and picked up the suitcase at her side (Fig. 3-12). *That* is style. It was clear she was giving her back the respect it required. I also realized that her correct technique stood out because so few people practice it.

When you pick up or put down your suitcase, don't bend over (Fig. 3-13). Bend your knees and keep your back vertical, as the airline attendant did. If you are carrying your suitcase with your right hand and get tired and want to switch to the left hand, don't pass it in front of you. Transfer it from one hand to the other in back of you (Fig. 3-14). Or if that seems awkward, put the suitcase down, turn around, pick it up with the other hand, and then turn around again. Or put it down, walk around to the other side of the suitcase, and pick it up with the other hand. Cumbersome? Perhaps, but better for your back than swinging that weight in front of you.

Better yet, put your stuff in two suitcases and carry one in each hand, thus loading your two sides equally.

Finally, why support the suitcase at all? Let the floor do it. Strap on wheels and pull your suitcase along behind you. The wheel was invented a long time ago. You might as well use it!

4 The Back at Rest: Basics of Sitting and Reclining

4

The Back at Rest: Basics of Sitting and Reclining

Fig. 4–1. The straight kitchen chair, though it's the choice of many a back pain sufferer, is not good enough.

CHAIRS

Sitting, especially sitting incorrectly in the wrong kind of chair, is harder on the lumbar discs than standing. The sufferer with low back pain usually chooses to sit on a straight kitchen chair. Such a chair is far from ideal, but it is a sad commentary on chair design that a straight kitchen chair is often better than anything else around the house (Fig. 4–1).

What chair design is kind to your disc? Careful experiments have been conducted to determine what features lower the pressure in the lumbar discs and decrease the activity of the back muscles (Fig. 4–2).

1. The backrest of the chair should be shaped to maintain and support the normal curve of the spine, particularly the natural lordotic curve of the lumbar spine. It is also helpful if the backrest of the chair is curved forward at the sides to give lateral support.

2. The backrest of the chair should be inclined backwards—the more inclined the better, the only limitation being that too much inclination means you are no longer sitting. You are lying down, and in no position to carry out whatever task your sitting position was intended to facilitate—eating, reading, working, writing, talking, or whatever.

3. The seat of the chair should be inclined upwards somewhat from back to front, that is, the front of the seat should be a bit higher than the rear.

4. The chair should have arm supports.

Fig. 4-2.   A well-designed chair: The backrest is shaped to support and maintain the normal curve of the spine; the sides are curved forward appropriately to give lateral support to the back; the backrest slopes backwards; the front of the seat is higher than the rear; arm supports to relieve the shoulders of the weight of the arms and to assist you in getting up from the chair.

Why these features? Let's consider each point in turn.

1. The normal shape of the discs produces the lordotic curve of the lumbar spine. If the chair you sit in eliminates the normal lordotic curve from the lumbar spine, it does so by distorting the normal shape of the intervertebral discs, and this causes the pressure in the discs to increase. One usually sits down for more than just a moment. Thus any increased pressure in the discs lasts for a long time.

2. If the backrest of the chair is inclined backwards, then a portion of the weight of the body is supported by the backrest, and the load on the vertebras and the discs is diminished. In the ultimate inclined position, namely lying down, the chair (the bed?) supports the entire weight of the body and the load on the discs results only from the remaining pull of the muscles.

3. The principal purpose served by inclining the seat upwards in front is probably to prevent the buttocks from sliding forward on the seat, for when you do slide forward, the normal lordotic curve of the spine is quickly altered and disc pressure increases (Fig. 4-3). Sliding can also be prevented by making the seat of non-slippery materials.

4. Most armrests support the weight of the arms, thereby relieving the shoulders and the back. They also help when it comes time to get up from the chair by providing you with something to push against.

Most chairs are incorrectly designed for prevention of low back pain. Too many so-called easy chairs and couches do precisely the wrong thing for sitting posture. They encourage the lumbar spine to curve in the wrong direction.

There are a few chairs on the market deliberately designed to maintain and support the natural lordotic curve of the lumbar spine. Your back knows that these are the true easy chairs and perhaps someday all chairs will be made with these design elements. But what to do in the meantime, and what to do with the furniture you now have and certainly can't afford to discard?

Fig. 4-3.   If you sit or slip toward the forward part of the seat, the normal lordotic curve of the spine changes into the reverse, a kyphotic curve, and disc pressure increases.

Fig. 4-4. A folded towel can be used as a lumbar support pad.

LUMBAR PADS

You can make yourself one of these to support the lumbar region of the spine. Fold a towel until it is six to eight inches wide and about one and one-half inches thick in the middle (Fig. 4-4) and then place it between the small of your back and your chair. A small pillow may do equally well. It may feel funny at first. In fact, you may even consider it uncomfortable. But that just means you're not used to it. Stick with it, and after about fifteen minutes, it should begin to feel less awkward. Use it regularly to help your back. Pretty soon you will miss it whenever you sit in a chair that doesn't have one.

Very few automobiles have well designed seats, shaped to give the proper lumbar support. Unfortunately, most are miserable and can cause you much grief on a long ride. Again, make yourself a lumbar pad and tie it in place on your car or truck seat with cord or elastic. You may be surprised how good your back feels after a long drive.

There are well-designed, ready-made lumbar support pads available on the market. However, you may have some difficulty finding them. In the Yellow Pages of your telephone book, look up chiropractors and physicians specializing in orthopedic surgery, and ask them to recommend a surgical supply store that carries lumbar pads. In larger cities, a few phone calls directly to surgical supply stores should locate the pads.

Get one and try it out. It may suit you very well, and you may wish to get some more so that there's always one around wherever you may happen to sit. Put at least one in your car. Take it, or your home-made variety, to the movies with you. Don't laugh. Two hours in a badly designed theater seat can be worse than two hours at a bad movie. It can cause a lot of subsequent misery, all quite unnecessary.

If you find yourself at a movie and, regretfully, have neglected to bring along your lumbar pad—improvise. If you're wearing a jacket or a sweater, take it off, fold it, and fit it into the small of your back. It's much, much better than nothing. It will

Fig. 4-5. The usual way of getting up from a chair. The back muscles, in supporting the bent-over back, put an increased load upon the discs.

help your lumbar spine retain its natural lordotic curve and help prevent low back pain.

RISING FROM A SITTING POSITION

You get up out of chairs dozens of times a day and probably don't give it a second thought—unless your back happens to be hurting at that very moment.

To get up from a chair, you have to move the center of gravity of your body so that it is over your feet which are usually in front of the chair. The simple, routine way is to lean forward and get up (Fig. 4-5). However, we should like to avoid bending the unsup-

Fig. 4-6. As you lean over and get up, push hard with your hands.

Fig. 4-7. If you slide your butt forward and your feet backward before getting up, you can get your weight directly over your feet without bending your back at all.

Fig. 4-8. To get up from an armchair, push with your hands against the arms.

ported body forward. It doesn't matter that you're sitting rather than standing. If you bend the body forward and do not otherwise support it, then the back muscles have to provide the support, and that imposes a heavy load on the discs.

There are several ways you can get up without overloading the discs. Lean over, but as you do so place your hands on your knees or thighs and push hard (Fig. 4-6). This supports your bent back with your arms. As your weight shifts to your feet, keep pushing, even harder, to straighten up your back with your arms.

Another way is to slide forward on your chair until you're sitting on the very front edge. If there's room

Fig. 4-9. At a table, push with your hands against the table.

Fig. 4-10. There's a limit to how far you can lean forward without tipping.

Fig. 4-11. When sitting, it's different—but not better. Don't do this.

under the chair, slide your feet back underneath it (Fig. 4-7) just until they are directly under your seat. Then your weight is over your feet and you can easily get up while keeping your back vertical all the while.

If the chair has arm supports, push down on them, again supporting your back with your arms (Fig. 4-8). You can even use your arms to push your whole body up into the standing position.

If you are sitting at a table, workbench, or desk, put your hands on the edge of the table and push down hard as you get to your feet (Fig. 4-9).

Perhaps you already do these things when your back hurts. The pain forces you to find a way. The difficulty is to get into the habit when there is no pain. Do it as a preventive measure.

You may not like the idea of complicating such a simple matter as standing up from a sitting position. It may take some attention at first, but after a while you will be using the proper techniques automatically without giving it thought.

Sometimes, after getting up out of a chair or out of bed, you may find that your back hurts as you try to straighten it up. Push outward hard with your abdomen; this will help you straighten up, with decreased or no pain at all.

AT THE DINING TABLE

Ordinarily, if you're standing with your feet together and knees straight, it is not possible to lean your rigid body too far forward without tipping over (Fig. 4-10). Your center of gravity will be moved forward of your toes and then there's no way to avoid tipping over except to move one of your feet forward. This happens even more readily if your arms are stretched out in front holding a heavy object. But if you are sitting in a chair, your feet are appreciably forward of your sacrum, and it is possible to lean far forward holding a weight in outstretched hands and still not tip over (Fig. 4-11). But that action imposes a large torque about the lumbar discs, requiring a huge amount of force by the back muscle to produce an

Fig. 4-12.   This can get you into trouble.
Fig. 4-13.   A vertical back is not enough if you're holding a load out front.

opposite torque. Overloading of the discs may result.

This sequence of events can happen to you at the dining table. If you pick up a heavy serving dish to pass to or from the opposite end of the table (Fig. 4-12), you will increase the load on the discs appreciably. It's better to get up and carry it around to the other side. Or make life easier by using a turntable or Lazy Susan, which will hold the serving dishes. It's easier on your back. You might also use a serving cart—a tea wagon—and wheel it around the table.

Fig. 4-14.   Balance the torque on your back by pushing with your arm.

Even if you don't bend your back but pick up a heavy pot of coffee at the table with your back vertical, the load in front of the body is not good for your discs (Fig. 4-13). Forget about table manners. Pick up the coffee pot with one hand, place the other arm on the table and push (Fig. 4-14). The torque of the coffee pot tending to bend the body forward will be balanced by the torque of your arm on your shoulder tending to bend the body backward, and you're home safe. You don't need to involve the back muscle and you don't overload the discs. It may seem a minor event, but all the little irritations add up and it's easy to avoid them.

AT A DESK OR WORKTABLE

Working at a desk or table has many of the same features, as far as the back is concerned, as sitting at the dining table. You want to minimize the torques that tend to bend the body forward. Pull your chair

Fig. 4-15. Pull your chair up close to the desk to eliminate unnecessary back bending.

close to the desk so that you don't have to bend your body forward unnecessarily (Fig. 4-15). But, of course, you may be sitting at the table in order to work on it, and you may *have* to bend over it. When you do, place your forearm or your elbow on the table and support your bent-over back with your arm (Fig. 4-16). If you reach across the table to pick up a book, telephone or some other object, the weight of the object at such a large lever arm distance calls for you to push even harder with the arm that is resting on the table (Fig. 4-17). And don't forget to equip your desk chair with a lumbar pad unless it has one already built into the design of the backrest—which is unlikely (Fig. 4-18).

Fig. 4-16. When you do bend over the table, support your back by pushing with your arm against the table.

Fig. 4-17. Definitely push with the other arm if you're picking something up across the table.

Fig. 4-18. Put a lumbar pad in your desk chair.

RECLINING

Lying down decreases the load on the spine appreciably because it no longer needs to support the weight of the upright body. The muscles acting on the spine can relax because there is no longer the need to maintain stability. During the day, when the compressive load on the discs is high, some fluid leaves the discs. At night, with the load greatly decreased, fluid moves back into the discs. You wake up in the morning an inch or more taller than when you went to bed because of the increased height of the intervertebral discs.

There is surprisingly little research on what kind of mattress is best to help prevent back pain. Much that is said is conjecture. The prevailing conjecture is that a reasonably firm mattress, not as hard as a board and not as soft as mush, is the best choice for providing the support needed to maintain the normal curve in the lumbar spine. As is probably well known to back sufferers, a soft mattress can be made firmer by placing a board between the mattress and the springs.

Lying supine, on your back, is an excellent position for achieving low disc pressure. It helps further to place something under your knees—a couple of pillows, a rolled-up and tied blanket, or a sleeping bag (Fig. 4–19). In this position, the thighs and knees

Fig. 4–19.   A good resting position.

are flexed. The muscle from the thigh bone to the pelvis is stretched less. It pulls less on the front portion of the pelvis causing less rotation, thus avoiding what might otherwise be an excessive lordosis of the lumbar spine—that is, too much curve.

If you don't put something under your knees, but just lie there with your legs out straight, you will probably soon feel the urge to cross your feet at the ankles. That may be your body's attempt to flex your leg, even if only a little bit, to lessen the stretch of a couple of muscles. After a while the ankle on bottom will hurt, the unflexed leg will want its turn and you'll cross over the other way. But it's not nearly as satisfactory, for relaxing the leg muscles and easing the pull on the pelvis, as placing something under the knees. Also, put one or two pillows under your neck and head—whatever feels comfortable.

Lying on your front is not a good position. It causes excessive lumbar lordosis.

In the course of a night's sleep, you might get tired of sleeping on your back and wish to change, or you may prefer a different position to begin with. Lying on your side is a good position, but again flex the thighs and the knees—now you don't need a rolled-up blanket to do so. The thighs should make an angle of approximately 135° with the trunk. That arrangement accomplishes three things in one fell swoop: It allows the normal lordotic curving of the lumbar spine; it keeps you from rolling over onto the front of your body; and it keeps you from rolling over onto your back. It's a relaxed and natural position.

The only problem is what to do with the "underneath arm." If you're lying on your right side, you

Fig. 4-20. On your side
—another good position.

need to find a suitable position for your right arm. The solution is easy. Bend your arm at the elbow so that your right forearm goes across your chest with your right hand ending up in the vicinity of your left shoulder. If you've never tried that position before— and it's amazing how many years we can sleep without finding all the positions—you may be surprised and pleased at how comfortable it is. Put the appropriate thickness of pillow under your head so that your head is horizontal, sloping neither up nor down from your neck—and you're all set (Fig. 4-20). Sleep well.

GETTING OUT OF BED

Take it slow getting out of bed in the morning. You're not really functioning yet. Use your arms and hands as much as possible to move your body around. Lying on your back in bed, push with your elbows and

Fig. 4-21.   Push yourself
up into a sitting position.

Fig. 4-22.   Push yourself
onto your feet.

hands against the mattress (Fig. 4-21) to get yourself
up into a sitting position, with your legs over the side
of the bed. Don't do a sit-up without using your arms
to push. Unassisted sit-ups raise the pressure in the
discs. Now, push yourself to the very edge of the bed.
Another push, keep your back vertical, straighten
out your knees, and you're out of bed, on your feet
(Fig. 4-22). Don't bend your back forward as you get
up unless you support the weight of your body with
your hands on your knees, on the night table, or on
something.

If you're having a bout of low back pain, the above
procedure may not be good enough. You may have to
support your bent-over back with your hands on

Fig. 4-23.   Support your
back by inching your
hands up your thighs.

Fig. 4-24.   Roll out of bed.
Fig. 4-25.   And push yourself onto your feet.

your knees and then straighten out your back by
working your hands up your thighs in little steps
(Fig. 4-23). Or, try a different way. Don't sit up at all.
Instead, roll out of bed onto your knees on the floor

(Fig. 4–24). Then with your hands on top of the mattress, push your back into a vertical position, push yourself onto one foot, straighten out your knees, and you're up (Fig. 4–25).

Be on your best behavior right after you get up out of bed. Do everything with the care of your back in mind. It is quite possible that your back is more vulnerable at this time because there is more fluid in the discs than at any other time of the day.

5

Those Backbreaking Chores: In and Around the House

5 Those Backbreaking Chores: In and Around the House

IN THE KITCHEN

Fig. 5-1. Don't hold the pot while it's filling up.

It is inevitable that, in the kitchen, you will frequently have to pick up heavy pots filled with water. Be careful how you do it.

When you go to the sink to fill a pot with water, don't hold the pot under the faucet (Fig. 5-1). It becomes a heavy load as it fills, held way out there in front of you. Even if you keep your back vertical, the forward-bending torque, because of the weight of the water, is too much. Set the pot down in the sink (Fig. 5-2) and let the sink hold it while it's filling. When you're ready to lift it out, turn 90° so that

Fig. 5-2. Let the sink do it.

Fig. 5-3. Lift it out at your side.
Fig. 5-4. Even if it requires two hands.

the side of your body is toward the sink, and lift it close to your side (Fig. 5-3). Even if the pot requires lifting with two hands, you can still do it at your side (Fig. 5-4). And carry it over to the stove that way.

When it comes to lifting the pot off the stove, it's the same story. If the pot is on a back burner, slide it

Fig. 5-5. Avoid bending over while preparing the food by working at a high counter.

Fig. 5-6. Or by sitting at a table.

Fig. 5-7. Another time to keep the back vertical and bend the knees.

Fig. 5-8. Or bend your back over, but support its weight with something other than your back muscles.

Fig. 5-9. Again—keep your back vertical.

forward first before lifting. Always bring an object close to the body before lifting.

You may doubt that this technique makes a difference, but it does. Hold a heavy pot in front of you and then move it around to your side. Without any conscious direction on your part, one set of muscles holding up your back, the back muscle, phases out and another set, the lateral muscle, phases in. Without any awareness on your part, the shift is made in beautifully coordinated fashion. But your lumbar discs know. The force on the discs is greater when the load is in front than when it is at the side.

When preparing food, try not to bend over. Either work standing at a high counter (Fig. 5-5) or sitting at a table (Fig. 5-6). When getting pots or utensils from a low cabinet or items from under the sink, don't bend your back. Keep it vertical and bend the knees (Fig. 5-7). Or if you do bend the back, support it with an arm by pressing down with one of your hands on a counter top or a cabinet door (Fig. 5-8).

When you mop the floor, also keep your back vertical. It isn't necessary to bend over (Fig. 5-9).

TAKING OUT THE TRASH

Once a week, many of us take the trash out to the curb. The easiest way is to wheel the containers out (Fig. 5-10). Lacking wheels, you can drag them out (Fig. 5-11), although you may not like the scraping and clatter. However, I suspect that most of us still

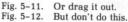

Fig. 5-10.   Use wheels.

Fig. 5-11.   Or drag it out.
Fig. 5-12.   But don't do this.

Fig. 5-13.   This may look
unusual—but it's easy on
your back.

lift and carry out the trash. If you must carry, *don't* carry the trash container in front of you (Fig. 5-12); carry it in back (Fig. 5-13) by its two handles. Simply put your two hands behind you, grab the container's handles, lift it up, and carry it out behind you. Your neighbors may laugh and ask what you're doing. Tell them. Even if they don't ask you, tell them anyway. They might end up thinking it's pretty clever.

If you're lucky enough to have a helper, you can carry the container between you—one on each side. That makes half the load and it's at your side, not in front.

MAKING THE BED

If the bedroom is big enough, leave space on both sides of the bed; it saves having to lean over. In many rooms, however, the bed is placed with one side against a wall, and the bed is not easily moved. If you lean over it to tuck in the sheets and blankets on the far side or to straighten out the covers in the middle, support the weight of your bent-over body with one hand placed upon the bed (Fig. 5-14) or upon the headboard. If you can get right up on the bed and do the job, that's better yet. To straighten yourself up after being bent over, remember to push hard with your hands against the bed. At the near side, to pull the sheet and tuck it in, bend your knees

Fig. 5–14. Support the weight of your bent over body with one hand or fist on the bed or on the headboard.
Fig. 5–15. Keep the back vertical.

or get down on one knee or both knees, and keep your back vertical (Fig. 5–15).

Best of all, if it doesn't bother you, *don't* make the bed.

THE LAUNDRY

Doing the laundry is an inevitable household task and usually means, among other things, that a loaded laundry basket is carried from one place to another.

It isn't possible to carry a laundry basket *close to the body* in front of you. Obviously you can carry it right up against your body but a laundry basket has an extended shape and even when one side is pressing against you, the rest of it is further away. Its center of gravity which is what counts, is about eight inches away.

You know by now what I'm going to say. Carry the basket behind you. It's easy enough to do. You just have to get accustomed to it and get over the feeling that it's a funny way to carry a laundry basket, or anything else for that matter. It's not the usual way, but carrying things the "usual way" doesn't help prevent low back pain. Carry it in a sensible way.

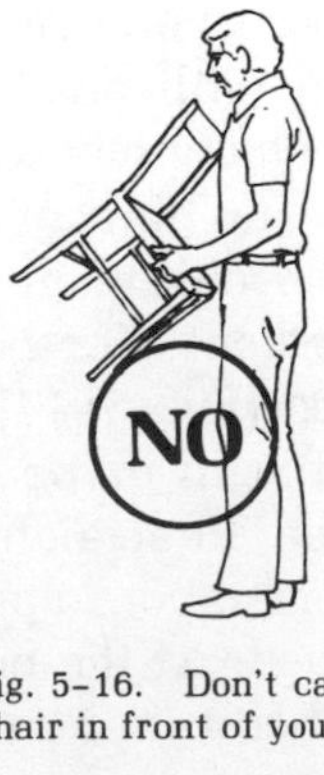

MOVING FURNITURE

Eventually, the time comes when we have to move some furniture around. It may be a relatively light task—moving chairs from one room to another. Or it may be a heavier task such as moving tables,

Fig. 5–16. Don't carry a chair in front of you.

couches, cabinets, or just lifting them up so you can slide a rug under a leg.

You may feel that a kitchen or dining room chair is light enough that no harm would be done in lifting it up and carrying it in front of you. But a chair, like the laundry basket, has an extended shape. It's not compact. Therefore, if you carry it in front of you, there's no way you can get its center of gravity close to your body. It's going to be way out there in front, putting stress on your back (Fig. 5-16).

Fig. 5-17.   Slide it.

Fig. 5-18.   Or carry it at your side.
Fig. 5-19.   Or behind you.

If the floor can take it, slide the chair without lifting it (Fig. 5-17). Otherwise, lift it at your side (Fig. 5-18), or behind you (Fig. 5-19). Or carry it over your head but watch out for doorways and hanging lamps.

Fig. 5-20.   Lift up furniture behind you, even if you must kneel down.

With heavier pieces of furniture, lift them up with your hands, but keep your hands in *back* of you whether you're standing up, bending, or kneeling down (Fig. 5-20). Figure 5-21 shows the *wrong* way.

If you and a friend are moving a table, the forward end is the place to be, because there you will have your back to the table (Fig. 5-22). If both of you want to do the right thing for your backs, then the person carrying the rear end of the table must consciously and deliberately turn his back to it and carry it that way. It is, admittedly, somewhat more awkward to use this technique, but it can be done, and it is much less awkward than being laid up in bed the next day.

Fig. 5-21.   Don't do this.

Fig. 5-22. It's the same story—if you have to carry a table, do it behind you.

OPENING A WINDOW

You can get into a lot of trouble just opening a double-hung window the wrong way. A double-hung window is the kind that slides up and down. Often they are very hard to slide. They stick in their tracks and you have to exert a large force to move them. If they are easy to move, if they fit loosely in their tracks, then you begin to worry about the winter winds pouring into the room around the sides of the windows.

Probably your usual way of opening the lower half of such a window is to walk up to it, pull up on the handles or push up on the upper frame of the window (Figs. 5-23 and 5-24). If the window is stuck, you may have to pull or push very, very hard. That's equivalent to trying to lift a very heavy weight in front of you. The harder you push or pull, the heavier the equivalent weight. By now, you know how bad that can be for your back. The torque tending to bend your body forward becomes very large.

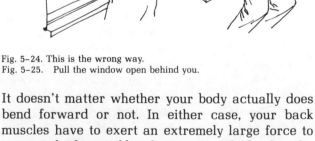

Fig. 5-23. Most people open windows either this way or as shown in Fig. 5-24. If the window is stuck, both ways are very bad for your back.

Fig. 5-24. This is the wrong way.
Fig. 5-25.   Pull the window open behind you.

It doesn't matter whether your body actually does bend forward or not. In either case, your back muscles have to exert an extremely large force to counter the forward bending torque. The load on the lumbar discs then becomes exceedingly high and you're inviting trouble.

There is a safe way to raise the window, and the guiding principle is, by now, familiar. Whenever

Fig. 5-26. You may have to get it started at your side.

possible, lift things behind you. Turn your back to the window and, if it has handles or is already slightly open, pull up on the lower frame with both hands behind your back (Fig. 5-25). If there are no handles, turn your *side* to the window and push up on the upper frame with one hand until the window is slightly open (Fig. 5-26), then turn your back to it and pull up behind you. You would do well to install handles on those windows that you open often. To close the lower window or open the upper window, face the window and pull it down (Fig. 5-27). Pulling downward in front puts no undesirable stress on your back. In fact, you may even get a little traction

Fig. 5-27. Closing the lower window.

Fig. 5-28. This is murder. Don't do it.
Fig. 5-29. But this is fine.

out of it. To close the upper window, turn your side to the window and push it up with one hand. Avoid pushing it up in front of you.

The worst possible window-raising situation is a stuck window, in front of which there is a table or a radiator. If you lean over the table or radiator and try to raise the window, you've had it (Fig. 5-28)—if not immediately, then the next day. Instead, move the table so that you can get to the window, or sit or stand on the radiator (Fig. 5-29). Otherwise, just let that window alone. Opening it is just not worth the consequences.

WORKING IN THE GARDEN AND YARD

It's not unusual, after a day of working in the garden or yard, to come down with back pain. Outdoors,

Fig. 5-30.   Squat.

Fig. 5-31.   Or get down on your knees.
Fig. 5-32.   Don't weed this way.

there are many ways of mistreating your back, particularly when you work for several hours as you probably do.

If you pick things off the ground, remember not to bend over unless you support your back by pushing with your hand on your thigh or knee or on something external that may happen to be around. Or keep your back vertical and bend at the knees.

If you're weeding, squat down (Fig. 5-30), or get down on one knee or both knees (Fig. 5-31). Wear knee pads or put a piece of foam under your knees if necessary. But don't stand there weeding with a bent-over back (Fig. 5-32).

Fig. 5-33.   Drag the branches behind you.

Fig. 5-34.   Use wheels.
Fig. 5-35.   Pushing a spade or a fork into the ground presents no problem.

If the winter has brought down a lot of tree branches to be removed, drag them behind you, while you walk forward (Fig. 5-33). Don't walk backwards while dragging them.

Rather than carry heavy loads around, use wheels:

a wheelbarrow, or garden cart, or a child's little red wagon (Fig. 5-34).

It's all right to push the lawnmower around, but pull it while walking backwards as little as possible and when you do, lean backwards, or turn around and pull it behind you.

There is no problem with using a spade or garden fork if you don't plan to lift anything. You push the spade or fork into the ground, either with your hands or a foot (Fig. 5-35) and then push downwards on the handle to loosen the soil. However, lifting up spadefuls of dirt or forkfuls of sod is quite another matter. There you can get into trouble. Read the section immediately after this one, about shoveling snow. It can be done—but the spadefuls should be kept behind you (Fig. 5-36)!

Fig. 5-36. But if you lift up a shovelful of dirt, be sure to keep the load behind you.

Light raking or hoeing is all right. But heavy raking, when you're really clawing at the ground or gathering up big loads of fall leaves, is troublesome. You pull the rake handle toward you and the rake tines, loaded with leaves, are dragging against the ground. That's a lot of pulling and it goes on for a long time. Every time you pull on the rake handle, your back muscles pull on your spine to keep it from bending forward. Your spine and discs get heavily loaded. It's also difficult to lean backwards while raking. You're more likely to be leaning forward, which only aggravates matters. I could say, turn around and rake behind you, but that's a very awkward arrangement and involves just too much undesirable twisting. It's appreciably more clumsy and more difficult than shoveling backwards. There's really no good way of raking leaves except to use an air blower or to leave the chore to the youngsters. What is needed is a differently designed rake, one that you can push rather than pull.

SHOVELING SNOW!

Shoveling snow gets an exclamation point because it is an activity to stay away from. You've heard that advice from those who tell you how not to get your heart into trouble. It's also good advice for not getting your back into trouble. Pushing the snow around is no problem (Fig. 5-37). The trouble comes from picking up those shovelfuls. That heavy load of snow, way out there at the end of the shovel at a long lever arm distance in front of you (Fig. 5-38), produces far too big a forward bending torque. It's worse if your back is bent over. But even if you keep your back vertical, the torque due to the load of snow is still acting on your back by way of your arms.

Get someone with a plow or a snow thrower to do it for you, or buy a snow thrower yourself. They're expensive, but you might be able to share the cost with the neighbors, and save several backs at the same time. When you use the snow thrower, let the engine do the work. That is especially important when you're backing up. Don't *pull* the snow thrower backwards. Put it in reverse and let it move under its own power even if it seems very slow. If *you* pull it, your back muscle has to pull on your spine to keep it from bending forward, and we're right back in the same old trouble again.

Despite the inadvisability of shoveling snow, sometimes you find yourself in a situation where you simply have no choice. It can be done safely by shoveling the snow in back of you! Turn your back to the pile of snow and with the handle of the shovel in front of you put the blade in back of you, pick up a load of snow (Fig. 5-39) and toss it backwards. Never bring the load in front of you. It's all right to bend your body forward and, in fact, you will have to.

Fig. 5-37. Pushing the snow should cause you no difficulty.

Fig. 5-38.   But picking it up like this is risking back trouble.
Fig. 5-39.   If you must shovel, SHOVEL IT BACKWARDS!

Bending forward will be offset by the load of the snow behind you and the two opposite acting torques may nearly balance, making it unnecessary for the back muscles to put on their extravagant show of force. If you have to, you can shovel that way and get away with it. Try it and see if anybody notices that you're doing it differently.

One caution: Try to twist your body as little as possible because torsion is not good for the discs.

AT THE MARKET— AND HOME AGAIN

Today in the United States, most food shopping is done in self-service supermarkets. You push around a shopping cart, load it up with groceries, and wheel it to the check-out clerk. There the groceries are unloaded and packed into bags. Then you either carry the bags home or they get wheeled out, loaded into your car, and driven home. At home, you unload them from the car, carry them inside, and put all the stuff away. A lot of lifting and carrying goes on. How can you accomplish the task and at the same time be kind to your disc?

Consider the shopping cart. At some markets, the carts are quite deep—to hold more—and at the check-out counter, you are expected to unload them yourself. At other markets, the bottom of the shopping cart basket is high enough to clear the top of the check-out counter and the clerk unloads it. If you have a choice (and the price is right), shop at the market whose carts have the shallower, higher baskets and where the check-out clerk routinely unloads it.

At some markets, you must wheel your groceries out to your car (in even deeper baskets) and unload them yourself. At other markets, your groceries are sent out on a conveyor belt and loaded into your car for you. If you have a choice, shop where they load your car for you.

Back to the market. As you load the shopping cart, particularly with the heavier items—potatoes, apples, sugar, flour, pet food—don't bend over to lower them into the basket. It doesn't matter that you are *lowering* the potatoes rather than *lifting* them. Unless you drop them in, you still have to support their weight. Turn your side to the basket and lower the items in along your side rather than in front of you.

At the check-out counter, lift them out the same way, by your side. If you purchased a carton of twelve bottles of soft drinks, beer, or anything else, and it has been placed in the basket instead of on top of it, then you have a problem. There's no way you can get that out yourself without bending over and lifting it out with both hands—and possibly injuring your back. It will take two people to pull the box up safely—one on each end, each of you with your lifting hand at your side or even somewhat behind you. When it gets reloaded for the trip out to the parking lot, don't let it go *into* the basket again.

Out in the parking lot, the groceries packed in paper bags go into your car. Put them on the seats rather than on the floor. If you have a station wagon, put them on the deck just inside the rear door. That way, when you get home and have to unload the car, you won't have to bend over to pick the bags up. It's much less desirable to put the bags in the trunk of the car, because unloading them later will probably require you to lean over and pick them up in front of you.

The whole idea is to arrange the bags so that you can unload and carry them into the house one at a time at your side, or two at a time, one on each side —but not in front. When it comes to that large, heavy carton, carry it behind you. Usually, you'll find a hand-hold slot on each side of the carton. Slip one hand in each and carry the carton in back of you, not in front.

The markets usually sell shopping bags with handles. They are a good investment and can be used over and over again. At the check-out counter, the clerk will put a paper bag inside the shopping bag and fill it up with groceries. The handles make the load considerably easier to carry and put in and out of your car correctly—one at each side with your back vertical. You may even put them on the floor of your car or in the trunk space without causing yourself trouble when you take them out. And if you walk home, bags with handles are a must, unless you use a cart or back pack. It is surprising that the bag with handles, such a simple aid, is so little used in most grocery shopping.

OPENING GARAGE DOORS

Fig. 5-40. Don't lift up a garage door in front of you.

Fig. 5-41. Pull it up behind you.

Fig. 5-42. And then at your side.

Many garage doors are of the overhead sliding variety. In a properly installed new door, a stretched spring supports almost the entire weight of the door, so that all you have to supply is a little extra force to overcome friction and move the door up or down. But after a while, the spring may fatigue, the wheels may not run as smoothly, friction increases, the door gets jammed, and you find you have to pull pretty hard to raise it. The same caution applies—over and over again—don't pull it up in front of you (Fig. 5-40). That is the same as lifting a heavy object in front of you. Turn your back to the door and lift it behind you (Fig. 5-41). If you've raised it a bit and cannot lift it any further that way, turn to the side of your body (Fig. 5-42)—but not in front—and continue.

Lowering the door is no problem, even if it is jammed. You can pull *down* as hard as you wish in front of you without doing any harm. But if the door moves too fast and you grab the handle and pull *up* to stop it, do so at your side, or somewhat behind you.

RIDING IN A CAR OR TRUCK

Once the vehicle is out of the garage a whole new set of problems faces you. Studies have shown that people who do a lot of driving, to and from work or in the course of their work, have many more incidents of low back pain than others. Let's consider the reasons.

Riding in a car or truck means sitting. Therefore, you immediately have all the problems of plain, ordinary sitting. Actually, it's worse than ordinary sitting, for the motion of the car is constantly jostling you. The muscles that are pulling on your spine to stabilize it have to pull even harder than usual in order to maintain stability under the continual impact of these disturbances. In addition, every time the car slows down, the body tends to lean forward. Every time the car swerves, takes a curve, or turns a corner, the body tends to lean to one side or the other, and the muscles are called upon to exert the extra pulls to counter these inertial tendencies of the body.

Whether you're the driver or a passenger, driving in general can be stressful to you and produce mental tensions that lead to muscular tensions.

Also while in the car you're immobilized. You can hardly move at all and certainly can't get up and walk about readily. You are confined to a sitting position and the spine may be under a greater load than usual from the large muscular forces, acting over a longer period of time than usual. The muscles themselves may even become strained from their continual, unrelieved, large effort.

A good seat becomes very important. If you're fortunate, you may have a vehicle with a properly designed seat—but it's unlikely. There are too few of them. A good seat must have a lumbar support—it must be shaped to fill in the small of the back and maintain and support the normal lordotic curve of the lower back. If your car seat does not have a lumbar support built in, you can buy or make a lumbar support pad (see Chapter 4).

A bucket seat—one that curves forward around the sides and snugly envelops the body—is helpful. It provides lateral stability and allows the muscles that would otherwise have to act to provide that stability to relax. However, even if your car has bucket seats, it should also have a lumbar support. If it does not, you may find that some of the ready-made lumbar pads are not suitable because they are designed to be used with a flat-backed chair. In that case, just make your own with a towel, as described in Chapter 4, and tie it on.

Stressful situations—icy spots on the road, a rainy night on a crowded fast highway, lack of confidence in the driver, fear of driving itself or whatever—will give you very tensed muscles. Sometimes that may be helpful—if it enables you to concentrate intently in a situation that requires it, and to get home alive. At other times, it serves no useful purpose. You just end up with a back that hurts. It's not as though you're going to move the car around with your very own muscles. What the car does will depend only on your alert and skillful movement of a few controls— and that does not require much muscular effort.

It's easy for me to say to you: RELAX. But it's also easier said than done. In many situations it may be difficult to achieve. Nevertheless: TRY TO RELAX. Be aware that the muscles pulling on your spine are unnecessarily tensing up. Perhaps just that awareness may help you consciously to relax—and a well-fitting seat will help.

As for being immobilized in the car, that's easy to deal with. On a long trip, don't try to set a time record. Stop every so often, get out, stand up, stretch and walk around. The trip will take a bit longer, but you'll be able to enjoy it more when you get there.

If you're on a vacation trip, then you also have luggage with you that you must load, unload, and carry. Remember to use your best technique for lifting and carrying luggage (see Chapter 3). Do have a good vacation.

Getting into and out of most cars with their low seats is usually rather awkward and cramped and can hurt if you have a bad back. It may provoke a muscle spasm. To get into the car, try this approach to the front seat: Open the door and with both feet on the ground, turn your back to the car and sit down on the seat. Then push your hands against the seat or the door frame or the steering wheel and swing your legs up and around, and you're in. To get out, do the same thing in reverse—you in reverse, not the car. Just before you actually stand up, slide over to the very edge of the seat, place your hands on your knees to support the weight of your bent-over body, and then straighten up by pushing with your hands and working them up your thighs.

Pulling on the hand brake can hurt. That same arm of yours that is pulling the hand brake backwards or upwards is pulling your back forwards and down, requiring your back muscle in turn to pull on your spine to hold it in equilibrium. To avoid the pull on your back, put your free hand on the dashboard and push. That decreases the necessity for the back muscles to act and avoids taxing the discs. (I must caution you that one friend, to whom I made this suggestion, reported back that he followed my advice and ended up cracking the dashboard! I hope your car is built more sturdily). As always, even if your back is not hurting at the moment, it's wise to follow the above procedure. We're interested in preventing back pain, not just easing the hurt after it happens.

When the car is in reverse, if your method is to turn around and look out the rear window, you may find that twisting is painful. Learn to back up using the rear view mirrors. Trailer-truck drivers are superbly expert at this. It takes practice. You can do it. But be extra careful; rear visibility is poor under the best of circumstances.

CHANGING A TIRE

Flat tires occur less frequently than they used to. But they still happen, and then you're faced with the job of putting on the spare. If you live in snow country, you also have the annual chore of putting on the snow tires in the fall and taking them off in the spring. Here are a few suggestions:

Jacking up the car requires you to push down on the jack handle. There is no problem on the downstroke (Fig. 5-43), but there is a mild problem on the way up, between downstrokes. You should be able to handle that by now.

It is very helpful if you sit on a low stool or box while removing and replacing the wheel (Fig. 5-44). That should be easy enough to do if you're at home, but it's somewhat more difficult if you're on the road. It's unlikely that you carry a stool in the car just in case you might need it. If you can find anything to sit on, do so. There's always a tire itself, but that, unfortunately, may be a bit too low. Lacking

Fig. 5–43. Pushing down on the jack handle should cause you no difficulty.

Fig. 5–44. Sit on a stool.
Fig. 5–45. Or squat.

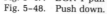

Fig. 5–46. DON'T bend over.

Fig. 5–47. DON'T pull up on the wrench handle.
Fig. 5–48. Push down.

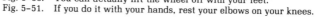

Fig. 5–49. If it's really tight, use your foot.

Fig. 5–50. You can actually lift the wheel off with your feet.
Fig. 5–51. If you do it with your hands, rest your elbows on your knees.

something to sit on, squat down (Fig. 5-45)—don't bend over (Fig. 5-46)—while working on the wheel.

To remove the wheel, you must loosen four or five nuts or bolts by turning them counterclockwise with the tire wrench. They may be on very, very tight because some rust may have formed on the threads, or someone may have used a wrench driven by compressed air the last time they were tightened. You may have to exert a large force to loosen them.

You're faced with a simple choice: Either pull up on the wrench handle to the right of the nut, or push down on the handle to the left of the nut. You may think it doesn't matter which choice you make—it's such a small detail—but it does matter. *Don't* pull up (Fig. 5-47). That would be like trying to lift a heavy weight. Instead, push down (Fig. 5-48). If necessary, you can even step on the handle with your foot (Fig. 5-49).

Once the nuts and bolts are removed, the next step is to lift off the wheel. If you're sitting on a stool, you can actually do it with your toes! Your feet are quite strong. Of course don't put your foot directly under the tire—just in case the car slips off the jack —but put your feet under the tire, one foot off at each side, and lift off the wheel (Fig. 5-50). If you lift off the wheel with your hands, make sure your elbows are resting on your knees (Fig. 5-51) so that your legs support the weight of the wheel. Whatever you do, avoid overloading your back by holding that heavy wheel out there in front of you.

The rest of the operation—lifting on the replacement wheel, tightening the nuts, lowering the car— is done in similar fashion, in reverse order.

6 Pain-Free Personal Care

6 Pain-Free Personal Care

DRESSING

When you put on socks, stockings, pantyhose, shoes, —try to do it with as little bending over of the back as possible. One way is to sit down on the bed, roll onto your back with one or both legs up in the air (Fig. 6–1), and put on your footwear that way. What do you care how it looks? It's fun and anyway you're in the privacy of your bedroom.

Fig. 6–1.   No extra load on the back here.
Fig. 6–2.   A bit more conservative.

More conventionally, sit on a chair, lean back, and draw up one or both feet (Fig. 6–2). When it comes to tying the shoelaces, put your shoe up on the edge of the dresser, if you dare (Fig. 6–3). Or, standing on the floor, bend your knees rather than your back to reach your shoelaces (Fig. 6–4). Or kneel down on one knee at a time.

It's becoming increasingly rare these days for people to wear galoshes, rubbers, or other overshoes in bad weather. But for those who are still interested in keeping their shoes dry and their floors untracked,

Fig. 6-3. Good for your
back but not so good for
the furniture.

Fig. 6-4. The back is vertical.
Fig. 6-5. Sit down to put on overshoes, or lean back against the wall.

pay attention to how you put overshoes on and off.
Do it sitting down or, if there is no place to sit, lean
against the wall and draw your leg up rather than
bend your back (Fig. 6-5).

IN THE BATHROOM

If you are not actually experiencing back pain at the
moment, it's probably all right to allow yourself the
luxury of no special rules in the bathroom. But if
your back is hurting, you'll discover quickly enough
that it's painful to lean over the sink to wash your
face or brush your teeth. What to do?

You can support your bent-over back with one
hand resting on the sink (Fig. 6-6). That only leaves
you one hand to pick up the soap and wash your face
—somewhat awkward, but not impossible. Alterna-
tively, keep your back nearly vertical, lower yourself
by bending your knees under the sink (if there is
room), and bend at the neck to bring your head over
the sink (Fig. 6-7). You can also wash your face
while standing straight (Fig. 6-8). You'll dribble
some water down, but if you're not wearing dress
clothes, there's no harm done. Water dries.

If your back is hurting, there's no way you can
wash your hair in the bathroom sink by yourself.
Either get someone to help or use the shower.

In the shower, don't bend down to wash a foot. In-

Fig. 6-6. You can support your bent-over back with one hand resting on the sink.

Fig. 6-7.   Or you can keep your back vertical and bend at the knees.
Fig. 6-8.   Or stand up tall and get a little wet.

stead, pick the foot up or get down on one knee. You should always have a non-skid rubber mat on the shower floor. You might also consider putting a stool in the shower so that you can sit down and reach your feet that way—without putting on a balancing act.

SEX AND THE BAD BACK

If you have a bad back, you know that it can interfere with your sex life. Sexual activity can bring on or worsen your back pain. The state of your back may, therefore, call for some modification in your style of sexual activity. For example, your partner should not rest his or her weight upon you. The added weight distorts the natural curve of your spine and will provoke the back muscles to contract. Neither of these effects are good for the back for they will increase the pressure in the discs.

Vigorous thrusting motions are accompanied inescapably by vigorous action of the back muscles and by distortion of the natural curve of the spine, once again imposing large stresses upon the spine.

In the most popular position for sexual intercourse, the woman lies on her back and the man is above her. Instead of resting the full weight of his body on

Fig. 6–9.   The man should avoid resting his weight upon the woman.

Fig. 6–10.   The woman should avoid resting her weight upon the man.

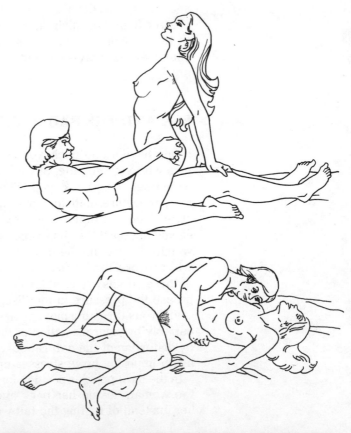

Fig. 6–11.   A good position for the backs.

hers, he should support his weight with his knees, legs, elbows, forearms, and hands (Fig. 6-9). That position also gives him greater freedom of motion.

In another popular position, the placement is reversed—the man lies on his back and the woman is above him. Even if she is lighter than he, and he stronger than she, it's not a good idea for her to sit or lie with her full weight upon him. She, too, should support her weight with her legs and arms (Fig. 6-10). And she will also be freer to move.

A position which is fine for both backs is shown in Fig. 6-11. The woman is on her back and the man is alongside her lying on his side. Neither one is on top of the other bearing the weight of the other. Each has one leg bent at the thigh and knee, each is between the other's thighs, and each has at least one hand free for fuller participation. They can lie together quite comfortably. It's a good position as far as the back is concerned. You will have to judge the sexual enjoyment yourselves.

These three positions give you the general principles by which you can evaluate the other nine hundred ninety-eight, or however many are in your repertoire.

Obviously, during a bout of actual back pain, you will have additional clues informing you what not to do. Depending on the degree of pain, you may find that almost any position and any movement of sexual intercourse hurts too much. That doesn't eliminate the possibilities for sexual enjoyment. There is warm, intimate, satisfying sexual activity, including orgasm—without actual intercourse. The woman's clitoris and the man's penis may be caressed and aroused and excited by a partner's fingers or tongue. Reports of recent years suggest that these forms of sexual activity are very widely practiced and enjoyed and that the orgasms and mutual warmth are very satisfying.

If, for whatever reason, they have not been part of your sexual practice, but you've had a secret curiosity or yearning about them, here's your opportunity. Blame it on your back and indulge yourself. You may both make some pleasing discoveries.

If you've had episodes of back pain in the past but

are not hurting at the moment, it's highly likely that you'll pay no attention whatsoever to anything said in this section. After all, it's not uncommon for many a rational consideration to be forgotten or ignored in the heat of sexual ecstasy. Nor is our knowledge of the human body so exact that anyone can *guarantee* to you that "if you do *this* your back will hurt, but if you do *that* your back will not hurt." I very much doubt that you will modify any of your usual sexual activities unless and until you have some hard evidence that modification may be necessary.

If and when you do develop back pain, which appears to be attributable to yesterday's session in bed, read this section over again. You may be more inclined to listen in the future.

7 The Children

7 The Children

HANDLING THE BABY

The baby is lying in the crib, crying, apparently in distress. You hurry to her, lean over the side rail, and pick her up for comforting. At that moment, the baby is all important and no thought is given to your back.

But other moments of baby care have less urgency. Don't bend over the side rail to pick up the baby (Fig. 7–1). Lower the side rail first, slide the baby over to the edge of the bed and pick her up, not with outstretched arms, but as close to your body as possible, and keeping your body as vertical as possible. Better yet, pick up the baby at the side of your body (Fig. 7–2). Learn the "football carry": The baby lying at your side, securely supported by your arm under her body and your hand under her head (Fig. 7–3). If the height of the crib's springs are adjustable, raise the mattress as high as safety will permit (Fig. 7–4).

If you pay attention to what is good for your back, the above procedure will become routine, and "second nature" to you. Even in moments of stress, you'll follow them without interfering with or delaying your primary and overriding concern for the baby.

When the baby is old enough to support her back and head upright, she can sit at your side straddling your hip (Fig. 7–5).

When you bathe or diaper the baby, do it on a high table so that you don't have to bend over (Fig. 7–6). If you bathe the baby in the regular bathtub, you should sit on a stool or kneel on your knees to minimize back bending.

Fig. 7-1.   Don't bend over
the side rail to pick up the
baby.

Fig. 7-2.   Pick the baby up as close to your body as possible.
Fig. 7-3.   The "football carry."

Fig. 7-4.   For an infant,
raise the mattress as high
as it will go—then you
won't have to bend as
much. Of course, as the
baby gets older, you will
have to lower the mattress
for safety.

Fig. 7-5.   The "hip straddle."
Fig. 7-6.   The high basinette for bathing the baby.

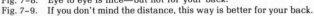

Fig. 7-7.   For a prolonged
period of time, let your lap
support her weight.

Fig. 7-8.   Eye to eye is nice—but not for your back.
Fig. 7-9.   If you don't mind the distance, this way is better for your back.

If you wish to hold your baby for a long time, sit down and rest her in your lap (Fig. 7-7).

BABY CARRIERS

There are two types of baby carriers you can use when you're out walking or shopping. One puts the baby on your back, the other puts the baby in a kind of sling in front of you. It's nice to have the baby in front of you (Fig. 7-8). You can maintain cozy face-to-face contact. But it's tough on your lower back and most parents agree that it is only practical for the first few months. As far as your back is concerned, the better place is on it (Fig. 7-9). You'll have to choose.

Actually, there is a way to have your baby in front and ease your back situation too—if you're willing to adopt a novel method. At the same time that you carry your baby in front, wear a small backpack (on your back of course) and fill it so that it balances the weight of the baby in front (Fig. 7-10).

Fig. 7-10.   Be different—have it both ways.

If you don't wear the backpack, your back muscles have to pull on your spine to balance the weight of the baby, and because they act at a much smaller lever arm distance from the lumbar discs, they pull much harder than the weight of the loaded backpack. You're actually easing the load on your discs by wearing the weighted back pack!

So, carry the baby in front and the supplies in back. If the supplies don't weigh enough, add something that does—a telephone book or two. Be daring —give it a try.

If your spouse is with you, it's going to look strange to an unknowledgeable onlooker that one of you is carrying the baby *and* a backpack, while the other is carrying nothing. But you can smile serenely in your knowledge that more can be less. Someone ought to manufacture and market a *one*-piece carrier that holds the baby in front and stuff in back.

PICKING UP THE YOUNG CHILD

During the first several years of a child's life, he

Fig. 7-11. Don't pick him up this way.
Fig. 7-12. Keep your back vertical.

Fig. 7-13. Don't lean over the gate to pick him up.

Fig. 7-14. Open the gate and do it right.

gets picked up from the floor many, many times. Year by year he gets heavier and heavier—and you get older. In general, the familiar rule applies: Don't bend over to pick him up (Fig. 7-11). Instead, reach him by bending your knees and keeping your back vertical (Fig. 7-12). Pick him up close to your body and, preferably, at your side rather than in front.

To safeguard a young child, an accordion-type gate is often placed at the top or the bottom of a flight of stairs or in the doorway between two rooms. Never lean over the gate to pick up the child on the other side (Fig. 7-13). (Unless you're seeking inspiration to write a book on low back pain.) Don't be lazy about it. Open the gate first so that you can get close to the child and pick him up in the proper way (Fig. 7-14).

The usual wooden playpen can be more of a problem than a gate. How to put the child in and take him out? It usually has no doors. If the child can stand, you can try lowering him in or lifting him out close to your side. But if the child is an infant lying on the floor of the playpen, that's a tough one. If the floor of the playpen is strong enough, you can climb in there with him and let him down or pick him up in the usual sensible way. But if the floor is not strong enough, and it probably isn't, you're stuck. I don't know any way it can be done properly. All I can say is: Do the best you can and then be on scrupulously good behavior with regard to everything else you do.

On some wooden playpens, the upper portion of one side is hinged and can fold down. That helps a

Fig. 7-15. Piggy-back is fine.

Fig. 7-16. Getting on— or off—your back.

little. Better yet are the nylon mesh playpens with one side that drops all the way down and permits much easier access to the baby. Keep it in mind when you're out shopping for a playpen.

PLAYING PIGGY-BACK

A "piggy-back" ride is just fine. So is a shoulder ride (Fig. 7-15). BUT—it *must* be done with your back vertical. Don't bend over. You must keep that in mind, particularly when the child mounts and dismounts. Sit down on a chair or on the bed and let him climb onto your shoulders or back from there (Fig. 7-16). And climb off the same way, in reverse. Never bend your back down to lower his feet to the floor, a chair, or the bed. And when you go through a doorway and you're afraid he might hit his head, don't bend your back—bend your knees.

8 Playtime

8 Playtime

COMPETITIVE SPORTS

Athletes are not immune to back troubles. No doubt you've heard of a star baseball player, tennis player, basketballer, golfer suffering with back pain. In addition to all the usual stresses upon the spine, the active sports participant has at least two more important ones to contend with:

1. When the trunk of the body twists around a vertical axis, each vertebra of the thoracic and lumbar spine rotates a little relative to the vertebra below it (and above it). It just takes a small rotation between each pair of neighboring vertebras to add up to a large overall rotation of the trunk. In that small rotation, the discs between the vertebras are twisted. Experiments on actual sections of the spine show that the annulus of the disc is particularly susceptible to developing tears when the disc is twisted. Repeated twisting of the body is a movement that occurs in many sports activities and puts the participant at added risk. If a tear occurs in the annulus of the disc, the tear itself may cause pain or the subsequent extrusion of the nucleus of the disc into and through the tear may cause pain.

2. In the heat of a game, a player may suddenly find it necessary to make an extreme effort, perhaps a great lunge to catch the ball or to hit it, with the muscles exerting maximal forces in an awkward physical position or movement. The added strain and stress on a lumbar disc may be too much for it and a disc will be damaged.

If your sports activities and your style of participation expose you to these additional risks, then you have a decision to make. Take the risk and continue the enjoyment of full and complete participation in the sports activity, or participate more moderately and lessen the danger to your back. My guess is that you'll take the risk until such time as you are laid low which may not happen at all. Only if you experience back pain, will you ease up.

BICYCLING

Fig. 8-1.   Back vertical—
no problem.

Many people are now bicycling. How does this activity affect the back? Basically, there are two types of bicycles in general use: one with standard handlebars, turned up, and the other with racing handlebars, turned down. In moderate biking, traveling at moderate speed on level terrain, it's possible to sit upright with your back vertical on either type of bicycle (Fig. 8-1). You don't have to push very hard on the pedals, and the involvement of the back is moderate. It stems mostly from the slight side to side shifting of your weight as the pedaling action shifts from foot to foot.

You may prefer to bend your back forward while bicycling, and on a racing bike that is the usual position. As far as your back is concerned, that's all right on either style bike as long as the weight of the upper part of the body is supported by the handlebars. That way, you don't require the back muscle to support your bent-over back. However, it may not be good for your fingers. When your hands push down on the handlebars, you compress the ulnar nerve in the palm of the hand and, after a while, this may cause loss of sensation and loss of muscular control in the fingers. It can be serious. If you do lean forward and rest your weight on the handlebars, use well-padded handlegrips or cycling gloves—and relieve your hands frequently by sitting upright.

Now, what happens when you try to pedal hard to go faster or to climb a hill? On a standard bike, kids

will often stand up over the forward pedal, letting
their whole weight push down on the pedal, while
the back remains essentially vertical. But adults
usually don't do that. On a racing bike it can be done
but it's somewhat difficult. The handlebars are too
low.

So how do you get enough weight over the forward
pedal while still sitting in the seat? By leaning forward and *not* supporting your weight on the handlebars. Next time you're out bicycling, try a little
experiment. Bend forward and support your bent
over back with your hands pushing down on the handlebars. Then start up a hill. As you begin to push
harder and harder on the pedals, you will notice
that you are pushing less and less on the handlebars. That means the handlebars are supporting the
weight of your bent over back less and less. What *is*
supporting your back? Your back muscles. But we
know that the back muscles, pulling at a small lever
arm distance from the lumbar discs, have to pull
very, very hard to provide enough torque to counteract the forward bending torque from the weight of
the upper part of the body, bent way out there in
front of the lumbar discs. As a result, the load on the
discs and spine may become excessive. You'll hurt.

It can even be worse than that. To push the pedal
down really hard with your foot, you'll find you actually have to *pull up* on the handlebars! That's like
bending over and picking up a heavy weight or pulling up a stuck window. And usually you'll bicycle
this way over an extended period of time. That's bad
for your back.

What do we learn from this? Moderate bicycling is
all right, but strenuous pedaling can cause trouble.
When you find you're leaning forward but hardly
able to press down on the handlebars, then you
know you're pedaling too strenuously.

Avoid steep hills. Faced with a choice between two
paths to the same hilltop spot, forego the challenge.
Take the long, gentle slope rather than the short,
steep one. If your bike has a gear shift, use the
lowest gear. You'll have more pedaling to do, but the
pedaling effort will be less. If traffic permits, go up

the hill criss-crossing from side to side; that effectively decreases its steepness. And finally, if you have no way around a steep hill, don't hesitate to walk your bike.

9

Pain, Injury
and Treatment

9 Pain, Injury and Treatment

EMERGENCIES

No matter how carefully you obey all the rules of good technique, there is not much you can do in sudden, unanticipated, emergency situations.

You slip on the ice and reflexively you respond, possibly with a tremendous muscular effort, a twisting motion, and an awkward position, in an effort to retain yor precarious balance. Even if you succeed in not falling, you may still end up with a hurting back, possibly the next day. The extreme muscular contractions may have overloaded the discs and the twisting motion injured the annulus. You may have strained a muscle or provoked a muscle spasm.

But it's not really something you can very well plan to prevent because your response at that instant is a reflex action—automatic and involuntary. Even if you should think about it ahead of time and decide that should you slip, you'll break the fall with your hands, without actually trying to prevent the fall. Nevertheless, when the occasion arises, you'll very probably flail about to try and prevent it.

Or suppose you're out walking with a friend who suddenly slips. Do you lunge to prevent the fall or just do nothing? Undoubtedly, you will lunge, though you may feel it later.

On the other hand, here's a different type of sudden incident, a small one, but one that can cause trouble—and is preventable. With your right hand you're carrying a large paper bag, loaded with heavy groceries or other purchases. The bag doesn't have handles, therefore you ought to be supporting

Fig. 9-1. You're asking for trouble—if one bag tears, its load will suddenly vanish.

it from underneath, lest it tear, but for some reason you're not—you've grabbed it at the top. To balance that heavy load on your right side, either your body is leaning to the left, or your left lateral muscles are pulling on your spine, or you're carrying another bundle with your left hand (Fig. 9-1).

Sure enough, suddenly the paper bag tears. Of course the contents spill onto the floor, but our concern here is with what happens to your body. When the load suddenly disappears on the right side, the upper part of the body begins to be pulled over to the left. Instantly, reflexively, the right lateral muscles contract, probably not a carefully measured contraction, but rather a massive response. And then the opposing left lateral muscles contract and together they maintain the stability of the upper body. But the extreme muscular contractions may leave you with some sore muscles and may overload the spine. You may end up with pain which takes several days, or more, to disappear.

Of course, once the bag tears, there's nothing you can do to check your reaction. But you can be careful not to put yourself in such a potentially vulnerable situation to begin with. That's what this little story is all about—not all accidents are accidental.

RELIEVING THE ACHES AND PAINS

My main purpose has been to help you *prevent* episodes of back pain from occurring. But suppose your back does hurt. What should you do then?

As soon as you feel a twinge of back pain—or pain in the buttocks, thigh, or leg—become very, very strict with yourself. If some appreciable time has elapsed since the last occasion when your back hurt, chances are exceedingly great that you have become lax in applying good techniques for lifting, carrying, and so on as described in earlier chapters. Perhaps you haven't read the book before or did not take it seriously.

Whatever the case, read it over and examine your many daily activities. Now is the time to apply, ever so much more diligently and scrupulously, the principles and suggestions explained earlier.

Get off your feet, get off your seat, and get on your back if you can manage it for periods of time during the day. Let the bed, couch, or floor, rather than your spine, support the weight of your body. Give your muscles a chance to relax and to unload the vertebras and discs.

If the pain is severe, then you *must* give your back a rest. Lie down on your back and put a bundle under your knees to flex your thighs and knees. If you have a lumbar support pad, place it under the lumbar region of your back (Fig. 9-2). And put a cou-

Fig. 9-2. Place a lumbar pad under your lower back.

ple of pillows under your neck and head. You will enjoy the relief. It may take a short initial period to get used to lying on the lumbar pad, but after that you should find it both comfortable and helpful.

If you're experiencing severe pain, lying on your back may not *always* be helpful. Sleep may become a problem. Pay attention to the pain. (I don't really have to tell you that; you'll pay attention to it anyway.) For a number of reasons, the pain may tell you that the usual helpful positions are not the best ones for now. Instead of lying on your back, try lying on one side or the other. Be as imaginative as you can and experiment with different positions. When on your side, try bending your head down toward your chest and drawing your knees up close to your chest (Fig. 9-3). Or draw up only one knee and stretch out the other leg. It may ease the pain for a while and then you may have to interchange the positions of the two legs, or find some other position. Try the other side. Maybe now lying on your back will work for a while, or even lying on your front. While severe pain persists, it must necessarily dominate the situation. It should strengthen your resolve, once it's over, to try to prevent a new episode of back pain.

Fig. 9-3. Try every position you can think of.

Turning over in bed—or any movement—may be painful. As soon as you start to move, even while you are merely preparing to move, the back, lateral and abdominal muscles may contract and aggravate the pain. They are not all needed for the job, but it's almost as though the muscles are not quite sure what's coming next and are mobilizing for action. Stop. Consciously let the muscles relax. Then start again, slowly, relaxedly. Use your hands and arms to assist the body's movement so that the other muscles can stay out of it.

You may want to consult your physician. It's possible that you're one of the small percentage of people with a specifically identifiable ailment for which some medical treatment other than rest is indicated. And even if not, your physician may prescribe a pain killer or muscle relaxant, if these are warranted, to ease your misery and hasten recovery.

Read over the section on getting out of bed (Chapter 4). Now more than ever, you will need to support your bent-over-back by pushing with your hands against your knees, and then straightening your back by inching your hands, one at a time, up your thighs, pushing hard with your abdomen all the time.

Sitting for too long a time may be very uncomfortable. Get up frequently and walk around. If you don't have a decent chair to sit in or one that you have fixed up with some kind of lumbar support, it may be better for you not to sit—or at least not until you have improvised a lumbar pad for yourself (Chapter 4).

The tension from constant pain and the anticipation of worse pain can be extremely exhausting. Lie down as frequently as you can, both for rest and for relief.

When you are feeling pain, it is unnecessary for me to tell you not to bend over for any reason without supporting your body with something other than your back muscles. The pain will stop you. It will actually protect you. If you don't violate its messages too much, in most cases you will recover in a few weeks although it may take as long as two months.

Once you're better, try to keep it that way. Not

only are the episodes painful, disabling, and debilitating, but you never know whether the next one may finally be more serious.

BED REST

In the overwhelming number of cases, the treatment for severe back pain is bed rest. Absolute bed rest, possibly with hospitalization, are sometimes necessary to make it work. One specialist suggests that the main purpose of traction is to make it look as though something is being done while really serving simply to keep the patient in bed.

Bed rest is a *conservative treatment*. Nothing drastic is done. Rest, pain medication—aspirin or a prescription drug—and a muscle relaxant are used to help break the cycle: pain provokes muscular spasm—causes more pain—provokes spasm and so on. In most cases, nature heals, and the hurt disappears or at least diminishes eventually, although it may take as long as a couple of months.

Because most patients get better without more active intervention, it becomes difficult to assess the effectiveness of other methods of treatment.

Drs. David Bachman and Howard Noble, in an article in *Modern Medicine*, comment half tongue-in-cheek: "Although ninety percent of back problems respond to rest, the problem has been assaulted with myriad approaches ranging from acupuncture to Zorroesque incisions. (In fact, treatment attempts can be categorized alphabetically: alcohol, baths, chiropractic, decompression, exercise, fusion, girdle, hysterectomy, injections, Jehovah, kneading, laminectomy, manipulation, neurectomy, opiates, psychiatry, quackery, rest, seance, traction, unguents, Valium, Xylocaine, yawns, and Zeus.)"

Ideally in medicine, one would like to test a treatment with a carefully designed experiment. Patients with similar symptoms are divided into two comparable groups. The patients in one group receive the new treatment that is being tested, the other patients receive some other treatment. But none of the patients knows which treatment he or she is receiving.

For example, if a new medicine is being tried out, one group receives the medicine, while the other might receive a similar looking and similar tasting concoction containing no active ingredients.

Sometimes the physicians, nurses, and therapists, dealing directly with the patients, also do not know which treatment they are administering. In the trial of a new medicine, someone other than the people handing out the medicine keeps track of which bottles have "real" medicine in them and which have fake. That is so the dispensators cannot inadvertently let the patients know who is getting what.

Finally, the patients' progress must be evaluated. If the original physicians did not know what they were dispensing, they may do the evaluations. But if they did know, then different physicians must do the evaluations in order not to be influenced by knowing which group got what.

For many reasons, it is exceedingly difficult to carry out such a test in the field of medicine and they occur infrequently. Not that all that rigor is always necessary. However, the history of medicine, including modern medicine, has many examples of diagnostic procedures and treatment methods which were generaly believed to be effective, both by physicians and by the public, but which turned out to be of dubious value or even harmful to the patient.

Controlled tests of low back pain remedies are scarce. Orthopedists have accumulated a great deal of experience dealing with the problem and such experience can prove very valuable in treatment. Yet it is not the same as determining what works and what doesn't through carefully designed tests and objectively gathered data.

All this is by way of saying: Treat your back pain conservatively unless your physician finds that it is due to a specific ailment for which there may be other, more effective remedies.

MASSAGE

If a skilled massage relaxes a muscle which is tensed or in actual spasm, then it clearly has the beneficial effect of relieving the pain of the spasm and relieving the load that the contracted muscles were imposing upon the spine. Enjoy it.

MANIPULATION

Manipulation therapy refers to the physical manipulation of the spine and surrounding muscles and tissues.

It's quite possible you've heard of someone who suffered a long time from back pain and nobody was able to help until one day he or she went to a chiropractor who manipulated the spine and in a short time the patient was in good shape—the pain was gone.

It is very difficult to draw any conclusions about the effectiveness of a mode of treatment from such anecdotal reports, even though events may have happened as told. What, specifically, did the manipulation purport to do? And was the manipulation directly responsible for the improvement, or only indirectly, by seeming to the patient to be an effective measure? Or did it just happen to coincide with what would have been a spontaneous natural recovery anyway?

Of course, quite understandably, you may not care how it works just so long as you get better. However, there are also other tales of the many who were not helped by manipulation or whose condition unfortunately worsened seriously after manipulation.

To many, there seems to be something almost magically (or is it, desperately?) attractive about setting the trouble right by somehow manipulating the spine back into its proper place. Perhaps it's the childhood recollection of a dislocated elbow and the skillful doctor who manipulated the bones of the arm back into place. Immediately the pain was gone and all was well. Or perhaps it's the common misnomer "slipped disc" which conjures up the image of a disc that has slipped out of its proper place between the vertebras and just needs to be manipulated back in. Systematic study is required to decide whether manipulation is a valid therapeutic technique.

In 1975, an international conference was held in Irvine, California to discuss the matter. Much of the conference time was devoted to discussing the need for an extensive study. There were reports on a few (too few) limited studies already conducted.

In one of these, the investigator found that, when muscle spasm was present, the most skilled manipulators appeared to be able to eliminate the spasm gently and thereby relieve pain caused by it. But in some cases the spasm soon returned, apparently signifying that the cause of the spasm had not been eliminated. Relief was temporary and the patients returned again and again. The underlying cause, whatever that may have been was not reached nor prevention achieved.

Another investigator found that manipulation produced a favorable initial response in a small fraction of the patients but that it was not possible to identify in advance which patients would benefit. And in the long run, it was no better than the use of a corset and only a little better than using pain-killing drugs such as aspirin.

CHYMOPAPAIN

This method is not a common one. It involves the injection, directly into the disc, of chymopapain—a substance which is supposed to interact with and eliminate the nucleus of the disc. It is intended for use in place of surgery for the removal of the interior of a disc. The success of this treatment method is still much in doubt; in fact, chymopapain is not used at all now in the United States because of its potentially fatal effects.

SURGERY

What about back surgery? If the pain is confined to the lower back, surgery is rarely needed. If the pain extends to a buttock, thigh, calf, or foot it is possible that a disc is protruding and pressing against a nerve root or that the annulus of a disc has ruptured and the pulpy nucleus has been squeezed out and is pressing against a nerve root. The trouble itself would be in the lower back but the pain might be experienced in the foot.

As you know, the various nerves carry messages from different parts of the leg to the brain informing the brain of what's going on down there, and carry instructions from the brain to the leg for different muscle fibers to contract. Nerve impingement on the sensory nerves in the lower back may affect sensations from the skin of the leg which your brain will interpret as pain in the leg. Or impingement on the motor nerves may make it impossible for you to contract certain leg muscles. Your physician can observe you and test your responses to various skin stimuli, muscular tasks, and movements of the limbs in an attempt to decide whether or not a ruptured disc is at fault and, if so, which disc. But the physician's diagnosis, at this stage, can only be tentative.

(By coincidence, as I write these paragraphs, I notice that one leaf of a large, handsome, hardy rubber plant, growing here in my study, has developed a brown spot, probably a diseased area. If nothing is done, it may spread to the rest of the leaf and possibly even affect the entire plant. Such a brown spot developed once before. Now, as then, I take a razor and, with only a little hesitation, cut out the diseased region. The cut edge exudes a white, sticky fluid for a while and then it clots. The surgery is over, and I fully expect that now, as before, the leaf will have been saved. Of course, it's possible that the leaf and the plant would have survived without the excision. But the problem was easy to locate, the surgery was exceedingly simple, it is a plant not a person, and I don't foresee any complications or ill effects. So why not cut? How different the human back!)

If a surgeon were to operate at this point, the chances would only be about seventy percent that the surgeon would find a ruptured disc and that it would be where the tentative diagnosis predicted. Seventy percent is not good enough for such an operation.

It is too early for surgery. Bed rest should be tried first for a period of time. There's time later for surgery should it still be necessary. There is no need for haste unless symptoms develop suggesting that a massive extrusion of disc material is pressing against a whole bundle of nerves in the spinal canal. Such pressure might cause widespread impairment of sensation or muscular activity in the lower part of the body, such as weakness of foot movement—a common complaint after herniated disc—or occasionally interference with bowel movement or bladder functioning. In such a situation, delay in relieving the pressure might result in permanent impairment.

Ordinary x-rays of the spine are of little help in diagnosing the cause of low back pain in most patients. In those few suffering from a fracture, a tumor, a vertebra which has slipped forward over the vertebra below, or a few other conditions, the x-ray will reveal the trouble. But ordinary x-rays will not show a protruding or ruptured disc. The nerves, spinal canal, discs, and any extruded disc material are all transparent to x-rays and do not show up on the x-ray film the way bones do.

The physician, examining a set of spine x-rays, may notice certain anomalies in the lumbar spine, that is, anatomical features which differ from his impression of what a healthy spine should look like. There may even be definite abnormalities. He may then decide to attribute the back pain to those anomalies or abnormalities. The difficulty is that there are too few spine x-rays of people without back trouble, for the obvious reason that such people don't have x-rays taken of their spine. It is therefore difficult to make a comparison with a "healthy" spine.

Even if the physician finds that the space between two vertebras has narrowed, it is not safe to conclude that the involved intervertebral disc is protruding, has extruded nuclear material, or is otherwise responsible for the back pain. There are many people, with a single narrowed disc, who do not have back troubles.

If the x-rays show the presence of a mild to moderate scoliosis—a lateral curvature of the spine—it may be tempting to seize upon that as the culprit. But studies of patients with scoliosis show very little correlation between scoliosis and back pain.

Myelography is an x-ray technique which does show whether there is extruded material present from a ruptured disc. A small amount of a special fluid that is opaque to x-rays and is heavier than spinal fluid is injected into the spinal canal, usually in the region of the suspected disc. By tilting the patient a little bit one way or the other while the patient is lying down, the fluid may be maneuvered around to the regions of the lumbar spine that the physician wishes to examine.

When the spine is x-rayed, the fluid will make the region in question appear white on the x-ray film. But if disc material is protruding and pressing against the spinal column or against a nerve root, it will displace the special fluid forcing it away from that immediate spot which will then print black on the x-ray film, contrasting with the adjacent white area. This record on the film is called a myelogram.

If the back pain and sciatica are really bad and do not improve with a good try at bed rest, then you and your physician have to consider the advisability of surgery. However, the prevalent opinion is that first a myelogram should be made to confirm a diagnosis of protruding or ruptured disc and to confirm which disc it is.

The myelography procedure may be unpleasant, there may be bad side effects, and there is a small possibility that something will go wrong. But myelography does decrease the probability of undergoing surgery only to find that the suspected disc is intact, that the rupture is at a location different from the site of the surgery, or after recovery that actually two discs were at fault but only one was operated upon because the other was not suspected.

Once the myelograms have confirmed a diagnosis of protruding or extruded disc, the decision has to be made to proceed with disc surgery or not. Some people may prefer to try more bed rest—perhaps a stricter regimen than before—or to put up with the pain and the loss of full functions rather than undergo the operation. Others may eagerly choose surgery to try and achieve relief from the incessant pain, exhaustion, and frustration. Many others fall between these two extremes. For them the decision is therefore more difficult. From my reading of the medical literature, the best medical advice appears to be: If the symptoms of sciatica are present, conservative treatment has not been helpful, and myelography clearly confirms the presence of a ruptured disc, you might as well proceed with surgery. Chances of subsequent relief from sciatica are very good if the surgeon actually finds the ruptured disc and removes it.

What is the procedure? The surgeon makes an incision in the back, cuts through various tissues—some muscle, ligaments, and some of the bone of the posterior part of a vertebra—in order to get to the intervertebral disc. Great care must be exercised not to injure any of the nerve roots running within or emerging from the spinal canal. If, as anticipated, the disc has extruded some of its pulpy nucleus through a tear in the annulus wall of the disc, the surgeon will first cut away the extruded material and remove it, and then cut out a piece of the annulus to gain entry to the interior of the disc and scoop out the nucleus. Here again great care must be exercised not to go too far accidentally and cut through the anterior ligament which covers the front of the disc, because just in front of the ligament run a couple of major blood vessels. Cutting into them would be very serious. Unfortunately, it sometimes happens.

After the operation, there is no longer any nuclear material in the interior of the disc to leak out and cause trouble. The fibrous tissue of the annulus is strong enough to support the load on the disc without the nucleus. However, you must continue to be careful not to overload the spine. You have been through a miserable experience, and the susceptibility of your discs to damage has been painfully demonstrated. It is not unusual, after a disc operation, for a second disc to cause trouble. By taking care you may prevent it. Be kind to your discs.

I must now enter some words of caution. Back surgery is a very serious operation. Things can go wrong. Do everything you can to be certain that the operation is necessary, and if it is, choose a highly qualified surgeon.

A subcommittee of the Congress of the United States, investigating the quality of health care in the country, reported in December 1978 that:

Unnecessary surgery remains a major national problem which requires urgent and accelerated attention. . . . unnecessary surgery continues to waste lives and dollars.

The evidence. . . demonstrates extensive variations in the quality of surgery being performed in this country.

Many surgeries end in misadventures (unexpected adverse events). One third of misadventures are preventable and a majority of these are surgeon related.

Keep in mind that your physician is your *adviser*, one whose advice should be given great weight. Nevertheless you, the patient, retain the responsibility for making the ultimate decision concerning treatments. Before consenting to surgery for the relief of back pain and sciatica, it is a very good idea to get a second opinion from another specialist in the field. Don't feel squeemish about asking for it— after all, you're about to undergo a major operation which will affect the rest of your life. If your physician has any doubts concerning the diagnosis or proposed course of treatment, he or she should welcome a consultation. Even a physician confident of a correct diagnosis should be able to appreciate your wish and need for confirmation.

The interpretation of the symptoms, tests, and even the myelograms is not always clear cut, and you don't want to be operated on if it is unnecessary or inappropriate. The eminent neurosurgeon, Dr. Bernard Finneson, in a book called *Low Back Pain* written for orthopedic surgeons, neurosurgeons, and other physicians, stated "[I am persuaded] that the largest group of treatment failures results either from improper evaluation or an inadequate trial of conservative management. . . it is startling to appreciate how meager and rudimentary is our knowledge of the subject [back pain]."

We make choices all the time, in medical treatment as in all the other activities of life. There are no guarantees. The decisions are made almost always with incomplete information, but we ought to do what we can to assure the chances of success within the present state of medical knowledge.

10 Exercise

10　Exercise

As you know by now, the emphasis in this book is not on exercise. There are many good exercise books around. There are also other back books that include exercise as the principal ingredient of a prevention program. Most YMCAs around the country offer an exercise program for back sufferers—The Y's Way to a Healthy Back.

While some exercises may help those with back troubles, other exercises may be detrimental. On the positive side, an exercised muscle will not get sore as readily as an unexercised one when you occasionally engage in an activity that makes extra demands upon the muscle. But a sore muscle is a mild complaint as far as back pain is concerned. It usually repairs itself in two or three days. It doesn't rate very high with any real connoisseur of back pain. It's also possible but not certain that a previously exercised muscle is less likely to go into spasm.

MISCONCEPTIONS

I've heard or read a number of popular statements which reveal some fundamental misunderstandings of the role of strong muscles in the mechanics of the back. I'll cite two of the most frequent:

"If your arm muscles are strong, they, rather than your back, will take some of the load when you lift things or carry them." This is not so. You need arm muscles to lift things and strong arm muscles are able to lift heavy things. But the arms transmit the

force and the torque to the shoulders, and the shoulders must be supported by the spine, its ligaments and its muscles. So it all ends up in the back; there's no diminution along the way. A beam, hanging from a steel wire at the end of a crane, needs a strong wire to hold it up. But no matter how strong the wire, it doesn't lessen the load on the crane one iota.

"If your back muscles are strong, they take some of the load off your back." Again this is not so. The back muscles pull on the spine. The harder they pull, the *greater* the compressive load on the spine. I'm not advocating weak back muscles such as may occur after an extended period of bed rest. But just don't call upon those back muscles to use their full strength because then they'll put too great a load upon the spine.

SOME EXERCISES TO AVOID

Fig. 10–1. Avoid this exercise—it raises disc pressure too much.

Some popular exercises actually raise the pressure in the intervertebral discs too much, and for that reason they ought to be avoided. Their effect may even be to produce back pain rather than prevent it.

I'll mention two such exercises, in particular. The first consists of bending the body forward and attempting to touch your toes or the floor (Fig. 10–1). This exercise raises the pressure in the discs excessively. The second is doing conventional sit-ups: Lying on your back with your legs straight or bent at the knees, you raise yourself up to a sitting position (Fig. 10–2). This too raises the pressure in the discs excessively. Toe-touches and sit-ups may be good for

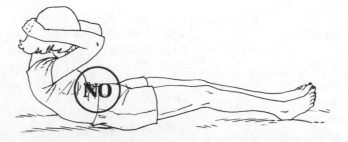

Fig. 10–2. Don't do this one, either.

stretching muscles and ligaments and strengthening muscles, but if your discs are vulnerable, they are *not* for you.

EXERCISES TO DO

Strengthening some muscles, especially the quadriceps, diaphragm, and other abdominal muscles, may be helpful in striving to prevent back pain. There are many exercises which have been designed to strengthen just those muscles. The ones described below are among the simplest while also being quite effective.

Fig. 10–3. Knee bends will straighthen your thigh muscles, making it easier to bend at the knees to pick things up.

The Quadriceps. One of the methods suggested earlier for picking things up from the floor was to keep your back vertical and to lower and raise the body by bending and unbending at the knees. This puts a larger than normal demand on the quadriceps —thigh muscles. You can strengthen them simply by doing knee bends (Fig. 10–3). Start with shallow knee bends and gradually make them deeper. Even more simply, if you adopt the practice of picking things up by bending at the knees rather than bending the back forward, the practice will be the exercise and your thigh muscles will get stronger.

The Diaphragm. On those occasions when you do bend over or you do pick something up in front of you, the pull which the back muscles need to exert and the consequent load on the discs can be decreased if the pressure in the abdominal cavity is increased. In fact this occurs reflexively without any conscious decision on your part. The appropriate muscles contract and the pressure in the abdominal cavity, in front of the lumbar spine, increases. But if you consciously acted to contract the muscles even more, the pressure in the abdominal cavity could also be increased, relieving the spine of more load. This calls for the strengthening of the appropriate muscles.

The abdominal cavity is bounded below by the muscles covering the bones of the pelvis, in back by the spine, in front by the abdominal muscles, and above by the diaphragm. The abdominal cavity, of course, is not an empty space. It is packed with organs—stomach, intestines, liver, kidneys, bladder, uterus, and more—all collectively referred to as the abdominal viscera.

The diaphragm is a thin sheet of muscle which separates the upper third of the trunk—the chest cavity—from the abdominal cavity. It is the principal muscle used in breathing. When relaxed, the diaphragm is dome shaped and reaches high up into the chest. When the muscle fibers of the diaphragm contract, the diaphragm flattens out, its central portion moves down and pushes against the abdominal viscera. The pressure in the abdominal cavity increases; the abdominal wall is pushed outward.

As surely as we breathe, the diaphragm is constantly being exercised—but only through a normal range. To exercise it further, and thereby strengthen it, take a moderate breath, hold it, and push the abdomen out (Fig. 10–4). You can push your abdomen against a belt, if you're wearing one, or against nothing at all. If I said, "Contract your diaphragm," you wouldn't know what to do. But that is what you're doing when you push your abdominal wall out. Hold it awhile, relax, and repeat. It's a very simple exercise; it can be done almost any place and any time—sitting, standing, driving—whenever you happen to think of it.

The Abdominal Muscle. When you push your abdomen out on its own it's actually being pushed against the abdominal muscles, and you also need to strengthen some of those to increase the pressure in the abdominal cavity. To do so, breathe out and force out as much additional air as possible by pulling your abdomen in as much as you can (Fig. 10–5). Hold it awhile, relax, and repeat. It's another simple exercise, and will strengthen your transverse and oblique abdominal muscles.

Fig. 10–4. Exercise the diaphragm further by pushing the abdominal wall out.

Fig. 10–5. Expel the last bit of air from the lungs by pulling in the abdomen. This exercises the transverse and oblique abdominal muscles.

11 Commercial Designs for a Healthy Back

11 Commercial Designs for a Healthy Back

RESEARCH INTO CHAIR DESIGN

In 1974, researchers in Sweden carried out a number of studies of the activity of the back muscles and the pressure in a lumbar disc while the subject was sitting. The chair in which the subject sat could be adjusted in a variety of ways. The backrest could be adjusted to change the angle of inclination between the backrest and seat. The inclination of the seat itself could be varied. And different amounts of lumbar support could be provided.

As we already know, the lumbar disc pressure when sitting upright is greater than when standing. The research findings showed that the activity of the back muscles and the pressure in the disc could both be reduced by increasing the inclination of the backrest. If, instead of using a straight chair, with a backrest making a 90° angle with the seat, one increases the angle to 100°, then muscular activity and disc pressure decrease. And the disc pressure decreases still further if the backrest inclination is increased to 110° or 130°.

We can easily understand why this happens. Remember, the spine consists of a large number of individual solid vertebras with adjacent vertebras connected to each other by an intervening, somewhat flexible disc. Left to itself, the spine could not remain upright. It would collapse. It's even worse when it has to support the weight of the entire upper portion of the body.

The muscles prevent the back from collapsing. You're not consciously aware of it, but the posterior back muscles, lateral muscles, and anterior muscles constantly pull on the spine in different directions to maintain the balance and stability of the spine. If you have ever fallen asleep (or watched others fall asleep) while sitting in an upright chair or other seat (subway cars are good places for this observation), you know that as you begin to doze off and the muscles relax, you invariably slump over, forwards or sideways.

The muscles must pull to maintain the stability of the spine, but in doing so they also increase the load on the discs. However when you sit in a chair with a backrest inclined backwards, then some of the muscles may relax and allow the spine to "collapse" against the backrest. The backrest is supporting you so there's no danger of falling over backwards, and gravity keeps you from tipping forward. Some muscles will still act on the spine to maintain sideways stability.

The decreased pull of the muscles results in less load on the lumbar discs. In addition, part of the weight of the upper body is borne by the inclined backrest, and that decreases the load on the discs still further.

The other important feature of the chair was the lumbar support. The experimenters used a very simple lumbar support pad protruding forward from the backrest a distance of 2 to 4 centimeters (3/4 to 1 1/2 inches), at the level of the third vertebra. They found that whatever the inclination of the backrest, the presence of the lumbar support decreased the pressure in the disc.

There is a reasonable explanation for this. The normal, natural curve of the spine is lordotic in the lumbar or lower back region. Lordotic means convex as seen from the front and concave as seen from the back. How does this shape come about? The vertebras are approximately cylindrical with the end plates approximately parallel to each other. If the vertebras were simply stacked on top of each other, the lower back would be only slightly curved. But they are not stacked directly upon each other. Between the vertebras are the discs and the two faces of each disc are not parallel. Instead, the normal shape of each disc is appropriately wedge-shaped to contribute most of the natural lordotic curve of the lumbar spine. If, for any reason, the natural lordosis of the lumbar spine is altered, either in the direction of increased lordosis or, as is more likely, in the opposite direction of decreased lordosis, that is, a flattening of the curve, then the shapes of the lumbar discs are altered. When the restraints of the ligaments and the pulls of the muscles squeeze the natural shape of a disc into a more or less wedge-shaped disc by shortening either the posterior or anterior height of the disc, then the pressure in the disc must increase.

When you sit down in a chair, the angle between the thighs and the trunk decreases to about ninety degrees. The muscles running from the front of the thigh bone to the pelvis get shorter while the muscles running from the rear of the thigh bone to the pelvis are stretched, pulling on the pelvis. This pull causes the pelvis to rotate backward, that is, the top of the pelvis moves backward.

The fifth lumbar disc sits on the sacrum which is attached rather firmly to the pelvis. When the pelvis, and with it the sacrum, rotates backward, the tilt of the fifth lumbar disc changes. If the back is to remain upright, the lumbar curve must flatten, and then the disc pressure increases.

If, however, a lumbar support is provided to move the lumbar spine back into lordosis, the natural shape of the lumbar discs is reestablished and the disc pressure decreases.

In some chairs, very commonly in use, the cushions of the seat and of the backrest, and the shape of the backrest actually permit and encourage the back to move toward kyphosis which is the reverse of lordosis. The convexity is toward the rear and the concavity toward the front. That, of course, means an even greater departure from the natural lordosis, and we can expect increased pressure in the lumbar discs.

The chair researchers also found a small additional decrease in disc pressure when the seat of the chair was tilted 10 degrees, with the front of the seat higher than the rear. Tilting the seat also means

that the backrest inclination is given an additional
10 degrees backwards and undoubtedly contributed
to the decreased disc pressure. With the seat tilted
upwards (or carved out in the rear so that the buttocks fit nicely into it) the buttocks are prevented
from sliding forward. If the buttocks do slide forward in any chair, you end up slumped in the chair
with a rounded back. The lumbar spine becomes
kyphotic instead of lordotic. Put plainly, the lower
back curves the wrong way and the pressure in the
discs increases.

The researchers explored many details, but I'll
single out just a couple of results. When the arms
were supported, either by resting them on a table in
front of the chair or on arm rests, disc pressure decreased. That is what we would expect. The spine
was relieved of the need to support the weight of the
arms.

When a subject, while sitting, lifted a weight, such
as a telephone, from the table at arm's length, disc
pressure rose markedly. Again, that is what we
would expect. But, as we have already discussed in
an earlier chapter, that pressure increase can be
prevented by putting the other hand on the table top
and pushing.

In the studies of muscular activity and disc pressure in the sitting position, one feature that was not
investigated was the effect of providing lateral support to the back. What happens if the sides of the
backrest are curved forward? In an automobile,
that would be called a bucket seat.

As we have already seen, when the backrest is inclined backwards, muscular activity and disc pressure decrease. There is less need for the muscles to
pull to maintain forward and backward stability of
the spine. But we can expect that there is still the
need for the lateral muscles to act to maintain
lateral stability—to prevent the spine from collapsing and the body from falling over to the left or to the
right. However, if the sides of the backrest are properly curved forward and wrap around the sides of
the body a little, then the backrest will maintain the
stability of the spine laterally as well as fore and aft.
We can expect the lateral muscles to relax and

thereby decrease the compression of the spine and the pressure in the discs still more.

If the backrest is made of textured material, rather than of smooth plastic as in some car seats, then it is not even necessary for the sides to curve forward. The friction between the backrest and a person's clothing should be sufficient to maintain lateral stability.

The role of lateral support has not actually been tested experimentally. However, qualitatively, the experimental results of the other theories of chair design have produced no surprises when compared with the predictions. That ought to give us some confidence as to what to expect.

AN EARLIER RESEARCHER

More than twenty years before Dr. Alf Nachemson and his group in Sweden did their comprehensive work on disc pressures and muscular activity in human subjects sitting in various chairs, researcher Dr. J. Jay Keegan, in the United States, had already come to the same conclusions about good chair design from his own studies.

Here are some marvelous quotes from one of Dr. Keegan's articles published in a medical journal.

One of the most common complaints of persons with low back pain is inability to sit in comfort, with difficulty in straightening the back on rising. This is particularly noticeable after long sitting in a lounge chair, an automobile, or a theater seat, all of which are supposed to be comfortable.

And a little further on:

Too often home-furniture manufacturers...have thought more of the luxurious appearance and sales appeal of the chair than of the user's requirements for comfort. The designers of supposedly comfortable lounge chairs have created monstrosities of overstuffed half-beds which provide neither a comfortable sitting nor a comfortable reclining position, permit no change of position, and are impossible to rise from without assistance.

He decides:

It seems time that recently acquired knowledge of the pathology of lower lumbar intervertebral discs be applied to the seating problem, and more correct fundamental rules be presented for the design of seats for the many persons with low back complaints.

That was in 1951. Today, there are still too few adequately designed chairs. We are burdened with chairs and couches which we must modify ourselves for our backs' sakes. Otherwise many of us experience immediate or subsequent pain.

Dr. Keegan did not measure disc pressures. The necessary techniques, instruments, idea, possibly even the willingness of live subjects were not then available. But he *was* concerned with keeping the pressure in the disc low to prevent extrusion of the nucleus pulposis.

With x-rays and photographs, he studied the shape of the lumbar curve in various body positions. He considered how different lumbar curves distorted the intervertebral discs and caused "hydraulic wedging pressure within the disc." And he was able to spell out the basic requirements for a comfortable and protective chair.

His principal specifications were confirmed twenty years later by actual measurements. He concluded that to yield lowered disc pressures, lumbar support is required to maintain the normal physiological lordosis of the lumbar spine, and the backrest of the chair should make an angle of at least 105° with the seat of the chair.

A SAMPLING OF GOOD COMMERCIAL DESIGN

There are a few commercially available items that I have found to be well designed as far as the care of the back is concerned. Unfortunately, the list is short. Of course, you'll have to exercise your own aesthetic judgment and any other judgments involved. My recommendation only covers their usefulness for your back.

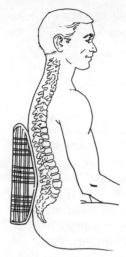

Fig. 11-1. The Posture Curve®.

Back Supports. In 1973, Dr. Bernard Watkins, a British orthopedist, patented a lumbar support pad. His design is very simple and straightforward—the pad fits the back. Yet no one, as far as the patent office knew, had designed one quite like it before.

Like the pads described earlier, this one fits between your lower back and the flat backrest of a chair. You can also place it under your back when you are lying down. It is doubly curved—to fit up and down along the lumbar spine and from side to side across the lumbar region. It is shaped to maintain and support the normal lordotic curve of the lumbar spine and also to provide sidewise stability. Because it is dimensioned for the average person, it will not fit everyone. However, it is flexible so you certainly don't have to be exactly average. As of this writing the pad is not generally available in retail stores in the United States, but it probably soon will be. It is called Posture Curve®(Fig. 11-1) and can currently be purchased from Body Care, Inc., 118 East 28th Street, New York, New York 10016, telephone 212-532-3998, and from several mail order houses.

Fig. 11-2. The Back-Huggar®.

One shortcoming of this lumbar support pad is that it is designed for use on a flat-backed chair. If it is used on a chair whose backrest is already curved laterally, then the curvature of the lumbar pad may become exaggerated and not fit the back and provide lumbar support quite as well. The folded towel lumbar pad, described in Chapter 4, will then do quite well as a substitute. In fact, it is not at all clear that the precise shape of Watkin's lumbar pad is necessary; an approximation to it may do just as well, as long as it provides support for the normal lordotic curve of the lumbar spine.

There is a similar cushion called Back-Huggar.® It does not fit the back quite as accurately as does the Posture Curve®, but it is adequate. It is available

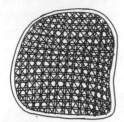

Fig. 11-3. The Invento Spine-Aid Back Rest has its own rigid frame.

Fig. 11-4. The S Range furniture with built in lumbar support pad.

Fig. 11-5. The recliner chair is helpful for the back.

from the Contour Comfort Company, 7240 Lem Turner Road, Jacksonville, Florida 32208 and is sold by some chiropractors (Fig. 11-2).

The Invento Spine-Aid Back Rest is a different type of back support. It does not curve significantly laterally, but it does provide support for the normal lordotic curve of the spine. It is bulkier than the previous two but has the advantage of its own rigid frame. It can be used on a chair with any shape of backrest. It is available from Hammacher Schlemmer, 147 East 57 Street, New York, New York, 10022, telephone 212-937-8181 or 914-946-7725 (Fig. 11-3).

Undoubtedly there are additional back supports on the market that provide proper support to the lumbar region of the back. Unfortunately, there are others that claim to be back supports but do nothing to maintain the normal curve of the spine. Beware— you'll only be throwing your money away.

Chairs. A variety of upholstered office chairs— swivel chairs, typist's chair, visitor's chairs, and others—have been manufactured which incorporate Watkin's lumbar support directly into the backrest. The seats are also well designed, being a bit softer under the buttocks than under the thighs and having a beveled front edge to avoid excessive pressure on the underside of the thighs and back of the knees. The chairs are called S Range (S for the shape of the spine!), and are available from Arenson International, 919 Third Avenue, New York, New York 10022, telephone 212-838-8880 (Fig. 11-4).

A recliner chair can be very helpful. The seat tilts up in front; the backrest tilts way back; and a leg rest comes up (Fig. 11-5). It's a good position for decreasing the pressure in the lumbar discs. There are many recliner chairs on the market, but few include a lumbar support, so that you still have to provide your own. It also helps if the leg rest is designed to keep your legs bent a bit at the knees. Shop around. You may find one that meets all the important specifications.

Automobile Seats. In Sweden, some of the research work of Dr. Alf Nachemson and his group at the Sahlgren Hospital in Göteborg has been supported in part by the Volvo Company, manufacturers of the

Fig. 11-6. The Volvo automobile has built-in, adjustable lumbar supports in the front seats.

Volvo automobile. Dr. Nachemson's group has investigated the pressure in the intervertebral disc and the activity of the back muscles in people engaged in a variety of activities and in a variety of positions, and seated in widely adjustable chairs. It is to the credit of the Volvo Company thay they not only helped support some of the research but took it seriously and incorporated the findings into the design of the seats in their automobile. The front seats are tiltable bucket seats with adjustable, built-in lumbar supports—probably the best seats in the automobile industry (Fig. 11-6).

I have made a survey of the seats in other automobiles. The seats in the Honda have a slight lumbar support. Almost all the cars manufactured in the United States have no lumbar support at all. The exceptions include: Lincoln, Cadillac, and Buick Regal, each of which has a slight lumbar support.

I have long wondered why car seats (and other seats) are so badly designed, principally with respect to lumbar support? I can think of one explanation: To the person unaccustomed to any lumbar support, a seat that has one built in can feel uncomfortable at first. And because car shoppers test the seats very briefly and make hasty judgments concerning their comfort, they don't give themselves a chance to adapt to the new feeling. On the contrary, because I am accustomed to lumbar support, if it's missing I feel an uncomfortable void in the small of the back.

12 Some Conclusions

12 Some Conclusions

Dr. John Knowles, a one-time director of the Massachusetts General Hospital, in discussing the book he edited, *Doing Better and Feeling Worse*, stated that "...for the most part, your health is in your own hands...people have to be 90% responsible for their own good health."

Some do seem to be accepting more responsibility for their health. More people are exercising: walking, jogging, running, swimming, playing tennis. Many have stopped smoking—although tobacco consumption has not decreased significantly, so it is also clear that new converts have taken up the habit. We're paying more attention to the foods we should eat and not eat—though at times it's exasperating to be confronted with the occasional reversals in medical advice which turn yesterday's meat into today's poison and vice versa.

Our spines have an inherent weakness in them. After the age of twenty, more or less, there is no longer a supply of nourishing blood to the the intervertebral discs, and the discs begin to deteriorate. As far as the present state of medical knowledge goes, there is nothing we can do about *that*. But we can and must accommodate to it and try to prevent the discs from becoming a source of pain, disablement, and possibly even worse—a site eventually requiring drastic intervention in the form of surgery, with results uncertain.

Be kind to your discs. Avoid overloading the spine, whether it be extreme overloads of short duration or small overloads of long duration. You're the only one who can do that.

Many people suffer their episodes of back pain without ever seeing a physician about it. And if they do, it may turn out that the physician is not sufficiently familiar with the biomechanics of the back or all the ways to avoid the overloading the vertebras and discs of the spine. And those who know can not possibly convey it all to you during the course of an office visit. Nor would you remember it.

That's a long chain of negatives, any one of which prevents you from getting the information you need to help yourself. That is why I have written this book —to introduce you to the mechanics of your back and to help you prevent back pain by pointing out how you can avoid overloading the vertebras and discs of your spine. Once you know what you *may* do, what you should *not* do, and what you should do *differently*, the rest is up to you.

It's worth the effort. It's a great joy to be able to move, to feel vigorous, to have your body back again, whole.

Glossary

Annulus fibrosus (annulus): The fibrous cylindrical wall of the intervertebral disc.

Anterior ligament: The ligament that extends along the front of the vertebras and the discs.

Back muscle: The group of muscles that runs back of the spine and tends to bend the spine backward.

Center of gravity: The point where the weight of a body can be considered to be concentrated for the purpose of determining the torque due to gravity.

Cervical spine: The seven vertebras and their discs in the neck region of the spine.

Cervix: This is the Latin word for neck. In medical usage, cervix refers to the neck or constricted portion of an organ of the body, e.g., the cervix of the uterus is the neck of the womb.

Conservative treatment: Essentially, bed rest and medication for the treatment of back pain.

Diaphragm: The flat sheet of muscle that separates the abdominal region from the chest region. It is the principal muscle used in breathing, and its contraction also increases the pressure in the abdomen.

Disc (intervertebral disc): The gellike fluid and the encircling fibrous tissue occupying the region between the vertebras and fastened to the adjacent vertebras.

Facets: Bony surfaces, on the rear portion of a vertebra, that match up with similar surfaces on the neighboring vertebras and guide the movements of the vertebras.

Foramen: The vertebral foramen is the large opening between the front and rear portions of the vertebra, that is, between the vertebral body and the vertebral arch. The aligned foramina of all the vertebras constitute the spinal canal.

The intervertebral foramen is the small passage, at the side of and between adjacent vertebras through which spinal nerves pass.

Herniated disc: Same as *ruptured disc.*

Intervertebral disc: See *disc.*

Intervertebral foramen: See *foramen.*

Kyphotic, kyphosis: Refers to a spinal curve that is convex toward the rear. The normal curve of the thoracic region of the spine is kyphotic.

Lateral muscles: The groups of muscles that bend the spine to the left or to the right.

Lever arm: The perpendicular distance (the shortest distance) from a pivot point to the line of action of a force.

Line of action of a force: A force is always exerted in some specific direction. If that direction is extended, both forward and backward, the line thus formed is referred to as the line of action of the force.

Ligament: A strong band of tissue that connects one bone to another.

Longitudinal abdominal muscle: This muscle runs along the front of the abdomen from the lower front bones of the pelvis to the ribs. When it contracts, it flexes the spine; that is, it bends the spine forward. It is also called *rectus abdominis.*

Lordotic, lordosis: Refers to a spinal curve that is convex toward the front. The normal curve of the lower spine, the lumbar region, is lordotic.

Lumbar spine: The five vertebras and their discs in the lower region of the spine immediately below the ribs.

Muscle: Fibrous tissue capable of contracting and pulling. When attached to bones, the muscle causes the bones to move.

Myelogram: The x-ray picture taken in a myelography procedure.

Myelography: A fluid, opaque to x-rays, is injected into the spinal canal and then an x-ray picture is taken. Any disc material that protrudes into the canal will displace the fluid and thereby reveal itself on the x-ray film.

Nerve: The fibers that transmit impulses (messages) between the nervous system (particularly the brain) and the other parts of the body.

Neurologist: A physician who specializes in problems of the nervous system. A neurologist or a neurosurgeon may be involved in back problems because of the possible impingement upon nerves.

Nucleus pulposis (nucleus): The gellike fluid in the center of the intervertebral disc.

Orthopedist, orthopedic surgeon: A physician who specializes in the preservation, correction, and restoration of the functions of the bones, the joints, and associated structures.

Pelvis: The bony structure between the lumbar vertebras and the thighbones.

Posterior ligament: The ligament that extends along the back of the vertebral bodies and the discs.

Protruding disc: A disc whose annulus protrudes or bulges into the spinal canal.

Ruptured disc: A disc whose annulus is torn and through which some of the nucleus leaks out and protrudes into the spinal canal.

Sacrum: The bone upon which the fifth lumbar vertebra rests.

Sciatica: A pain radiating from the back into the buttocks and the legs.

Scoliosis: A lateral curvature of the spine.

Slipped disc: Ruptured disc is the more correct description.

Spinal canal: The canal formed by the alignment of the openings (the foramina) in all the vertebras. It encloses the spinal cord.

Spinal cord: That part of the central nervous system contained in the spinal canal and from which the spinal nerves emerge.

Spinous process: The rearmost bony portion of each vertebra. The "buttons" you feel down the middle of your back are the spinous processes.

Spondylolisthesis: (If you can pronounce this one, you qualify as a Radio–TV sportscaster.) The forward displacement of a vertebra over the one below, usually of the fifth lumbar over the sacrum, or the fourth over the fifth.

Supine: Lying on one's back, face upward.

Thoracic spine: The twelve vertebras and their discs in the middle region of the spine. The twelve pairs of ribs are attached to these vertebras.

Torque: A measure of the tendency of a force to cause a body to turn about a pivot point. The torque is equal to the force multiplied by the lever arm.

Torsion: Twisting.

Transverse processes: The bony lateral projections, on the rear portion of the vertebras, to which ligaments and muscles are attached.

Vertebra: One of the bones of the spine.

Vertebral body: The large, forward, cylindrical, weight-bearing portion of the vertebra.

Vertebral foramen: See *foramen.*

A Short Bibliography

A FEW OTHER BACK BOOKS

Finneson, Bernard E.: *Low Back Pain*. J. B. Lippincott Company, Philadelphia, 1973. For the medical profession.

Lettvin, Maggie: *Maggie's Back Book*. Houghton Mifflin Company, Boston, 1977. A nice breezy style—includes exercises.

Levy, Joanne P.: *Ouch! My Back is Killing Me!* Exposition Press, Hicksville NY, 1978. The author draws upon her experience as a physiotherapist.

Root, Leon and Kiernan, Thomas: *Oh, My Aching Back*. Signet, New York, 1973. Abundant anatomical and medical information—includes exercises.

Rush, Anne Kent: *The Basic Back Book*. Moon Books/ Summit Books, Berkeley CA, 1979. A very funny book.

SOME OF THE PIONEER RESEARCH ARTICLES

Andersson, B. J., Örtengren, R., Nachemson, A., and Elfström, G.: Lumbar disc pressure and myoelectric back muscle activity during sitting. Studies in an experimental chair. *Scandinavian Journal of Rehabilitation Medicine* 6: 104–114, 1974. An investigation of the relation between various chair features and disc pressure.

Bartelnick, D. L.: The role of abdominal pressure in relieving the pressure on the lumbar intervertebral discs. *Journal of Bone and Joint Surgery* 39B: 718–725, 1957. The title speaks for itself.

Bradford, F. Keith: Certain anatomic and physiologic aspects of the intervertebral disc. *The Southern Surgeon* 10: 623–629, 1941. Simple lever analysis demonstrating the huge force on the disc when lifting a weight with outstretched arms.

Keegan, J. Jay: Alterations of the lumbar curve related to posture and seating. *Journal of Bone and Joint Surgery* 35A: 589–603, 1953. Sound recommendations for the design of decent chairs.

Markolf, Keith L. and Morris, James M.: The structural components of the intervertebral disc. *Journal of Bone and Joint Surgery* 56A: 675–687, 1974. A comparison of the compressive strength of the annulus alone to that of the intact disc.

Mixter, William J. and Barr, Joseph S.: Rupture of the intervertebral disc with involvement of the spinal canal. *New England Journal of Medicine* 211: 210–215, 1934. The authors conclude that rupture of the intervertebral disc is not uncommon and may be a cause of back pain and of sciatica. (The authors acknowledge a monograph on the intervertebral disc by G. Mauric, Masson et Cie, Paris, 1933, containing similar conclusions.)

Nachemson, Alf and Elfström, Gösta: Intravital dynamic pressure measurements in lumbar discs. *Scandinavian Journal of Rehabilitation Medicine,* Supplement No. 1: 1–40, 1970. Additional and more comprehensive measurements of the pressure in the lumbar discs of live subjects during various activities and positions.

Nachemson, Alf and Morris, James M.: In vivo measurements of intradiscal pressure. Discometry, a method for the determination of pressure in the lower lumbar discs. *Journal of Bone and Joint Surgery* 46A: 1077–1092, 1964. The first of the famous measurements of the pressure in the lumbar discs of live subjects.

Subcommittee on Oversight and Investigation of the Committee on Interstate and Foreign Commerce, House of Representatives: Surgical Performance; Necessity and Quality. Committee Print 95–71, U.S. Government Printing Office, Washington DC, 1978.

The report concludes that there is too much unnecessary surgery.

SPECIAL MENTION

Benedek, George B. and Villars, Felix M. H.: *Physics, with Illustrative Examples From Medicine and Biology.* Vol.1, *Mechanics.* Addison-Wesley Publishing Co., Reading MA, 1973. A marvelous book, and cited here because it stimulated me to inquire further into the subject of low back pain.

Index